D0045307

THE MARVELWOOD MAGICIANS

WITHDRAWN

THE
MARVELWOOD
MAGICIANS

DIANE ZAHLER

BOYDS MILLS PRESS

AN IMPRINT OF HIGHLIGHTS

Honesdale, Pennsylvania

Text copyright © 2017 Diane Zahler
All rights reserved.
For information about permission to reproduce selections from this book, contact
permissions@highlights.com.

This is a work of fiction. Names, characters, places, and incidents are products of
the author's imagination or are used fictitiously. Any resemblance to actual events,
locales, or persons, living or dead, is entirely coincidental.

Boyds Mills Press
An Imprint of Highlights
815 Church Street
Honesdale, Pennsylvania 18431

Printed in the United States of America
ISBN: 978-1-62979-724-3 (hc)
ISBN: 978-1-62979-918-6 (e-book)

Library of Congress Control Number: 2017937875

First edition
The text of this book is set in Bembo.
Design by Tim Gillner
10 9 8 7 6 5 4 3 2 1

FOR STAN:
I MISS YOU EVERY DAY

CHAPTER 1

The name of the game was Frog Jump. It looked simple enough: players took a rubber frog and placed it on a platform, then smacked the platform with a mallet to try to make the frog leap over the pond onto a metal lily pad. Mattie knew it was rigged, like all the games in the arcade, but her brother, Bell, had been studying it and playing it at fairs all summer to figure out how to win.

"Hey, Dane," Bell said to the man in charge. "Can I play?"

"Again, kid? For free?" the man said. His arms, where they showed below the sleeves of his dingy white T-shirt, were completely covered in a tangle of tattoos, but he had a nice smile. "You think I'm in this for my health?"

"Please?" Bell wheedled.

The man grinned and handed Bell a limp rubber frog.

Bell took his time positioning his frog, studying it from one angle, then another. He whacked the mallet down hard. The frog flew across the water and landed right on a lily pad.

"We got a winner, folks!" Dane called out, and people turned to look. "Choose your prize, kid!"

Bell jumped up and down, thrilled, and Mattie wondered how he could still be so excited about winning one of the moth-eaten stuffed animals they gave out at the arcade. Then again, just a year ago, she'd been that excited, too. She didn't know quite when that feeling had stopped.

"You take it, Mattie. It's for you," Bell said. Dane held out a little turquoise bear to Mattie, and her hand brushed his. Right away Mattie could read what he was thinking, as clear as anything.

Shouldn't let the kid play for free, but they'll never miss one stupid bear, he thought, smiling that sweet smile. *The idiots didn't even miss the money I took. If they paid me what I'm worth, I wouldn't have to do it. It's not really stealing.*

Mattie stared at him. "Stealing is stealing," she said before she could stop herself.

Dane flushed, and Mattie took a step back, alarmed by the anger in his eyes.

"What did you say?" he demanded, flexing his biceps so that the painted snakes that wound around them seemed to twitch.

"Nothing. Sorry," Mattie muttered. She poked Bell and turned to leave.

"Wait a minute, you!" Dane said. He started to come around the frog pond toward them, his face red and furious.

"Run!" Mattie shouted to Bell. She grabbed his hand, and they took off.

They sprinted through the arcade crowds and zigzagged around the booths. A minute later they entered the chicken and rabbit barn, panting, and tried to mingle with the other fairgoers. Mattie let go of Bell's hand, glad that because he was family, she couldn't read his mind. Still, she knew what he'd be thinking: *Oh boy, Mattie's done it again!*

They made their way past overexcited toddlers begging to play with the rabbits, and cages filled with hundreds of chickens, from the ordinary barnyard variety to striped black-and-white hens to the crazy kind with the leg feathers that looked like the flared pants Mattie had seen in photos from the 1970s. She kept looking behind her, but there was no sign of Dane. They'd lost him—for now. Then she turned to Bell.

He was gone.

"Bell," Mattie said, and then a little louder, "Bell!" She didn't want to draw any attention. Luckily, the people around her were enthralled by the chickens, and they didn't notice when Bell reappeared. He wavered a little, his sandy hair and copper-colored eyes indistinct at first, then solid. His freckles were last to appear.

"Don't do that!" she hissed at him.

"Sorry," he said. "I thought Dane might be following us."

"If he was, he'd have seen you go," Mattie pointed out.

Bell shrugged. He didn't spend much time thinking about getting found out. "So what did you hear?" he asked. "What did he steal?"

"Money," she said. "He's been skimming money off the game for months. A lot, I think. He's sure to get caught. What an eejit." That was their father's word for *idiot*.

"He was nice to me," Bell said regretfully. "He let me play for free."

"I know," Mattie said. "I'm sorry. Now he's probably going to make trouble for us. Why can't I just keep my mouth shut?" She was furious at herself for putting Bell in danger. Carnies were always unpredictable. She should have known better.

Bell patted her arm. "You can't help it. Come on, let's go back to the wagon. It'll be time for Da's act soon."

"Don't tell Maya and Da what happened, okay?" Mattie begged, and Bell pretended to zip his mouth closed.

They passed the food stands where people sold ice cream and sausages and every fried thing on a stick imaginable. A trio of girls holding Italian ices turned to look at them. "Nice outfit," one of them said to Mattie. The girl's hair was a golden waterfall across her shoulders, and her clothes were tight and trendy. Her two friends had dark hair, and neither was as pretty and perfect as she was. Mattie had a feeling that the blond girl had planned it that way.

"Thanks," Mattie said evenly, though she knew the girl was making fun of her. Mattie's old skirt was much too long for her; its hem swept the dust. Her top was an embroidered peasant blouse, and around her shoulders she clutched a paisley shawl. She refused to wear one of her mother's gold-embroidered saris when she performed, so after weeks of arguments, the skirt and shawl were what they'd finally settled on.

The blond girl snickered, and Mattie brushed by them, turning to watch as they tossed their barely touched ices into a trash can and linked arms. What would it be like, to spend a day with friends, to wander around with nothing to do? Those girls probably went home every night and ate dinner in a real dining room, with parents who wouldn't let them have their dessert until they'd eaten their vegetables. She felt a stab of longing so strong that she had to stop, a hand on her chest, to catch her breath.

"Come on, Mattie. We'll be in trouble if we're late," Bell warned. The girls had disappeared into the crowd. Reluctantly, Mattie followed as Bell led her through the fair.

Shrieks came from the rides in the distance, the giant Ferris wheel and the pirate ship that swung back and forth, and Mattie's absolute least favorite, the Kamikaze, spinning its two little cabins on either side of a giant rotating rod. She'd ridden it once when she was Bell's age and thrown up for an hour afterward. She hadn't been on a ride since. Even now she had to turn her eyes away from the Kamikaze when she walked past or she risked feeling a little sick.

The wagon came into sight. It was their home on wheels, their school, and their workplace. From the outside it looked rickety, about to fall apart. Once it had been bright green, but now the paint was faded and peeling. On the side was a sign, and it wasn't in much better shape than the wagon itself.

THE MARVELWOOD MAGICIANS

it read, in flaking gilt paint. And below, in smaller letters:

MAYA THE FORTUNE-TELLER
SIMON: MASTER OF ILLUSION
MATTIE THE MIND READER
THE DISAPPEARING BELL

Maya was Mattie's mother, Simon her father. Bell was her younger brother, and she was Mattie the Mind Reader. The sign didn't mention the youngest Marvelwood, Tibby, but she was only four. Mattie knew that she'd be up there soon enough.

They could see Maya standing out front, her thick black hair blowing in the breeze, her hands on her hips. She looked annoyed, and when she saw them, she called, "Mattie, hurry up! You have clients!"

"Oh no," Mattie moaned, and Maya frowned.

"You are a member of this family, Mathilda Marvelwood," she scolded. "You have to do your part."

"Stop nagging me!" Mattie retorted. "I take care of Bell, and Tibby when you need me to. I help Da. Why isn't that enough?"

"Hey, I take care of myself," Bell protested.

Maya sighed. It was a sigh Mattie had heard a thousand times. "You have a talent, Mattie. It is part of who you are, just like mine and Da's and Bell's and Tibby's are part of us. You cannot just pretend it does not exist."

"Oh, I could," Mattie assured her. "If you'd let me, I definitely could." She knew she was stepping over the line. Her mother had a quick temper, though no one would guess it watching her dreamy fortune-telling act.

This time, though, Maya held back. She just pointed to the wagon. "They have already paid."

Mattie rolled her eyes and climbed up the steps, hitching up her skirt and neatening her hair, long and dark like Maya's. She pushed open the door and saw that three of the seats around the table were taken, leaving only the last for her. And then, to her dismay, she realized that the customers sitting in them were the three girls she'd passed by earlier. They must have really hurried to get to the wagon before she did.

"See, I told you it was her! Mattie the Mind Reader," the

blond leader said in a mocking voice. "Oh, Mattie, would you read my mind? Please?" She made her eyes big and round and innocent, and she and her curly-haired friend laughed. The other girl looked embarrassed.

Mattie took a deep breath, willing herself to be calm. These were clients, nothing more. She'd never have to see them again after today.

"Yes, of course I will," she said, hoping her voice sounded serene. She closed the door, shutting out the noises of the fair. She walked to the empty chair and sat. Then she passed her hands over the table as if she were pushing away any stray thoughts that might have been lingering there. Clients liked this, she'd learned. Her movements were slow and graceful; she'd practiced them with Maya for years. The room was dark and quiet, and the smell of sandalwood was hypnotic.

"I'll have to read you one at a time," Mattie said to the blond. "Otherwise, the thoughts will be too confusing. And I'll need to touch your hand."

The girl put out her hand, and Mattie laid her own over it. She was flooded by thoughts. *What a loser!* came first, and she clenched her teeth. Then: *The last fair didn't have this, it's kind of stupid. Used to be more fun at these things. So sick of hanging out with these jerks. Maybe next year I'll go with Ben.* Mattie saw an image of Ben, a handsome boy with dark hair kicking a soccer ball. He looked friendly. He looked like the kind of boy Mattie thought about sometimes, the kind of boy she'd never dare talk to if she actually met him.

"Ah, Kira," Mattie said in a low voice, ignoring the twitch in the girl's hand when she spoke her name. "I see a schoolyard. There's a boy in a soccer uniform. He's cute, with dark hair. I see that you like him, this Ben." The girl jerked her hand away.

"Wait, how did you know my name? How did you know about Ben?" she demanded.

The other girls exchanged looks. "Maybe she heard us talking," one of them suggested, the one with curly hair. "That's how they do it, I think. They eavesdrop, and then they use that." Kira pursed her lips, her eyes suspicious.

"Do me next!" the curly-haired girl said, and Mattie turned to her and touched her hand. *Kind of cool. I wonder if anyone can really read minds? How about a test—hey, girl, Mattie the Mind Reader, read this! I kissed Ben myself, and Kira doesn't know!*

Mattie hated when this happened. People were always trying to test her. If she repeated what she'd heard, there'd be a huge fight, and screaming and crying probably, and usually she was the one who ended up getting in trouble. If she stayed quiet, then the person was convinced she was a fake. Sometimes they even asked for their money back.

"I see that Bette has some secrets," she murmured. "I see that . . . no, they're foggy. You keep your secrets well, Bette. I think . . . maybe you kissed someone."

The third girl, the one with short dark hair, squealed, and Kira said, "Who? Wait, you kissed someone and didn't tell us? Who was it?"

Bette stared at Mattie, and then said, "It was my brother's friend. You know, Jake. At that party in June." Mattie looked back at her without blinking, and Bette flushed.

"My turn!" cried the third girl, and Mattie leaned across the table to touch her hand. Her thoughts were all over the place, admiration for Kira mixed with jealousy and even a little fear, and a desperate wondering about whether she'd be invited to a sleepover someone was having the next weekend. She seemed nice, not mean like the other two.

Mattie thought that in another world, another life, they might get along.

"I see strong feelings for friends," Mattie said, "and a worry about an invitation."

"What will happen?" the girl asked, her eyes wide in her round face.

"Sorry, I can't read the future," Mattie replied. "I can only see what you're thinking right now." That wasn't exactly true. If she really concentrated, she could read people's memories, their fears and longings. But she usually tried not to concentrate. She didn't want to know.

"Wow." The girl smiled shyly. "Do you like doing it?"

Mattie paused. Nobody had ever asked her that before. "Sometimes," she said honestly. "It can be really . . . interesting."

"Is that it?" Kira demanded. "Are you done?"

"Do you want me to say more?" Mattie asked her. With her eyes, she tried to convey that she knew what Kira thought about the other girls. Even in the dim light, Mattie could see Kira redden. She stood up, and Bette and the round-faced girl—Wendy—stood, too.

"What a freak," Kira said. "You're a whole family of freaks." The others followed her out, but Wendy paused at the door and turned back. Mattie looked at her, outlined in brightness from the sun outside.

"Thanks. Bye," Wendy said, and then she was gone.

Mattie sighed. It was hard to imagine what it would be like to know girls like that. Some of them were so nasty, once she read their thoughts, that she was glad she didn't have to deal with them anyplace but in the wagon. But the ones like Wendy—well, it would be nice to have a friend like her. To go to school and the mall and to wear clothes like other girls wore. To have a normal life and a normal family.

Mattie neatened the cloth that covered the table and started to fold up the chairs. It was almost time for Da's act. The objects he materialized were only illusions, but they made people gasp with awe. Sometimes he amazed even her, creating a gorgeous vase he'd seen on a museum postcard, or a wizened head from a *National Geographic* article on headhunters, almost real enough to touch if you dared. The best was when they worked together. Mattie would go through the crowd before the act started, touching people gently to see what was in their thoughts. Then she'd whisper to Da, and he'd make a beloved toy from someone's childhood appear, or a necklace that had been lost for years, or the dress that an old woman had worn the night she fell in love.

The girls had left the wagon door open, so Mattie heard when the shouting began. Maya was yelling, "No, I will not let you speak to her! You have no business with an eleven-year-old girl!"

"Oh, I've got business, lady," the other person snarled back. With a start, Mattie realized it was the carnie, Dane. "Your kid sticks her nose where it doesn't belong, did you know that?"

Mattie sidled over to the door and peeked out. Dane stood in front of Maya, towering over her. Beside him were two equally large and nasty-looking men, their heads shaved and their bulky biceps tattooed. Maya had an arm around Bell, and Da was hurrying toward them, Tibby on his shoulders. You couldn't tell by looking at them, but it was only Da's grip on Tibby's legs that kept her from rising into the air.

"Mama!" Tibby cried, her eyes—one brown and one blue—round with wonder. "That man has a snake on his arm!" She pointed at Dane.

"What's going on here?" Da asked.

"They said—," Maya began.

"Your daughter's been saying things she shouldn't have," Dane interrupted. "Spreading lies about me. I think it would be a real good idea if you all just left."

"I see," Da said, looking at the three men. Each of them outweighed him by about fifty pounds. "I see," he said again. "Well, it just so happens that we were planning to leave shortly."

"Now," Dane suggested, and Da sighed.

"I meant now," he agreed. He swung Tibby off his shoulders, whispering what Mattie knew was a command to stay rooted to the ground, and mounted the stairs to the wagon.

"Shhh," he said when Mattie started to speak, to explain and apologize. "Let's pack up."

Silently and swiftly they got ready to go. There wasn't much to do: they secured the things in the wagon that might fall over and break, and then Da backed the truck onto the wagon hitch. The three men watched without speaking, their arms folded across their broad chests. Maya strapped Tibby into her booster seat in the backseat of the truck, and Bell and Mattie climbed in on either side of her. Maya and Da took their places in the front, and Da turned the key. Luckily, the motor caught, though it coughed and the truck shuddered.

It had happened again. The freak family was on the move.

CHAPTER 2

"I'm sorry," Mattie said miserably as they drove away in a cloud of dust. "I saw that he was stealing, and I—I know I should have kept my mouth shut. I didn't think."

"I do wish you had," Maya said. Even the back of her head looked tense.

Mattie flared up. "That's not fair! You do the same thing in your readings all the time! Remember that lady from last week? The one you told not to accept her boyfriend's proposal? She was furious with you! It's so hard not to say anything!"

"Now, now," Da said, trying to soothe them. "You're two sides of the same coin, you both."

"We are not," Mattie said automatically. She hated it when Da compared her to Maya.

Maya turned in her seat to look at her. She didn't seem as mad anymore. "I know how hard it is," she said. "It will always be difficult for you, as it is for me. The boys and Tib have it easier."

"What did Mattie do?" Tibby piped up. "Is she in trouble again? Was it that bampot who was yelling?"

A bampot was an idiot, in Scots. Tibby called almost everyone that; she loved the sound of it.

"Mattie's not in trouble," Da said. "It was just time to go. And now it's time for you to do some lessons—you missed your history on Friday because we were setting up."

"A very good idea," Maya agreed. "We were talking about . . . what? The Oregon Trail?"

"Wagon trains!" Bell exclaimed. "Indian attacks!"

"The Donner Party," Mattie muttered, but Maya heard her.

"Mattie," she cautioned, with a glance at Tibby.

"Sorry," Mattie said, though she was pretty sure Tibby would love the story of how the Donner group had to eat each other to keep from starving in the mountains on their way to the West.

Maya and Tibby went through the alphabet first, with Da making letters materialize and hang over the backseat and Tibby trying to grab them and name them. Da could make an *S* with a forked tongue like a snake or a *B* that buzzed like a bumblebee, and Tibby shouted the letters, hissing and buzzing along with them.

Then Maya talked about the Oregon Trail, and Bell and Mattie looked at illusions of covered wagons, and petticoats, and the sunburned faces of pioneers. Sometimes Da concentrated so hard on the picture he was materializing that the car swerved, and then the illusion would pop like a bubble and disappear as he pulled back into his lane.

"But why would they want to go west?" Mattie asked. She'd never understood it. "How could they leave their homes and everyone they loved to go somewhere that they knew was going to be hard and dangerous and horrible?" She knew the Ingalls family did it in the Little House stories, which she loved, but it wasn't the traveling parts of those books that she read and reread. It was the family parts, where they spent the long winter evenings playing music in front of the fire or worked together in the fields. And most of all, it was the parts in the houses—the log cabin in the Big Woods, the house Pa built on the prairie, even the dirt dugout on the banks of Plum Creek. The places where they settled and stayed.

"That's what people do," Da said mildly. "Humans have always explored. From Europe to America, west to California, up to the moon. It's ingrained."

"Not in me," Mattie said, half under her breath.

"Enough, Mattie," Maya warned.

"Would you really want to live just in one place?" Bell asked her. He couldn't believe it, no matter how many times Mattie told him she would. "Wouldn't you be bored? Nothing new to see, nobody new to know? Everything the same, every day?"

"I think it would be amazing," Mattie said softly. "Living in a real house, going to school . . ." But Maya sighed in annoyance, so she dropped it.

They ate sandwiches at a roadside rest stop as night fell. The moon, round and orange, came into view over the treetops that lined the narrow road leading south. The truck couldn't make it on the superhighways, or even the regular highways. When Da pushed it over forty-five miles an hour, it developed a cough and started to shake like an old man with the flu. So they stuck to the smaller roads wherever they went. Mattie was glad. There was a lot to see out the window, usually—houses and towns and sometimes even people walking along the side of the road. She watched the moonlit view slide by, and after a while, with the clanking of the truck engine and the regular breathing of her brother and sister as a lullaby, she fell asleep.

She woke to quiet. Not just quiet, but *too* quiet. The sound of the truck motor had stopped. She could hear the summer locusts screeching outside, and the hood of the truck groaned as Da opened it to peer in at the engine.

"What's wrong?" Mattie whispered.

"It just . . . stopped," Maya said, running her hands through her thick hair, usually smooth and neat, so it stood out crazily around her head. "Not a bit of warning."

Mattie rubbed the sleep from her eyes. "Uh-oh," she said. "Maybe we're out of gas?" That had happened before. The gas gauge wasn't too reliable.

"Not this time," Maya said.

Mattie eased the door open and climbed out. In the gleam of moonlight and the sharper glare of the headlights, she peered under the hood with Da. She had no idea what she was looking at, but she could tell that things weren't supposed to be smoking in there.

"That doesn't look good," she noted.

"No," Da agreed. "Might be a fair idea for us to get out of the truck."

Maya woke Bell, and Mattie helped him stagger out as Da lifted Tibby, still sound asleep, from her booster seat.

"What now?" Maya asked. She sounded very tired.

"We walk, I suppose," Da said. "I am sorry, love. I thought the last fix would hold awhile."

"Not your fault," Maya said in a brisker tone.

"Can't you just image up a new engine?" Bell asked, whiny at being awakened. "I don't want to walk."

Da gave Bell a half-frown, half-smile. "You know that wouldn't work. They dinna stay." He pointed, and for a moment, a car engine hung in the air between them, as real-looking as the one in the truck. Then it disappeared.

"We passed a sign not far back with a town name on it," Maya said. "So we should get to the town before long. Surely they will have a mechanic."

And a motel? Mattie wanted to say, but she knew better. They had the wagon, so they didn't need to waste money they couldn't spare on a motel. But they were walking away from the wagon, and she really, really wanted a shower.

"Wait," she said. "I need to change. I'm not going to any town dressed like this." They'd left the fair in such a rush that she was still wearing her mind-reading outfit.

"You look fine," Maya said impatiently.

"I do not!" Mattie protested. "Just let me get my jeans and a T-shirt. It'll only take a minute."

"It's all right, Maya love," Da said to Maya, handing Tibby to her, then smoothing down her wild hair. "I'll get them—just in case the truck goes up." The engine wasn't smoking anymore so Mattie didn't think there much danger of that, but Maya let him go.

"They're in my trunk, on top," Mattie told him.

He was back quickly with the clothes, and Mattie changed behind the wagon, tossed her skirt and top inside, and locked the door. Then they set off on foot down the road.

The moon lit the way or it might have been impossible. Bell had a flashlight attached to an all-purpose knife that he always carried, but its narrow beam barely touched the huge darkness around them. Everyone was exhausted, and things rustled in the brush on the side of the road, making Mattie jump. She was just about ready to sit down on the asphalt and refuse to take another step when she saw a sign down the road. *Welcome to Frog Creek*, it read in the unsteady glow of Bell's flashlight. *Population 2,464.*

They staggered on past a row of houses with wraparound porches and huge trees in their front yards. All the windows were dark. Everyone was sound asleep. Then they were in the town, really just a street with some stores lining it. There were a few streetlights, but the shops were closed up tight—except for one.

"Look, it's a diner!" Bell said, excited. "Can we get something to eat? I'm so hungry!" Mattie realized that she was, too. The only food she'd had was those sandwiches, hours before.

"I could eat," Da said, shifting Tibby's weight. So they headed toward the diner, one of the sort Mattie liked best, old-fashioned with a silvery metal front.

A bell over the door tinkled when Bell pushed it open, and a woman sitting at the counter swiveled on her stool to look. She had a round face below a halo of white hair, and her cheeks creased into a hundred wrinkles when she smiled. It was the kind of smile that you had to smile back at.

"Are you open?" Da asked, lowering Tibby to the ground. She scrabbled like a kitten to keep her hold on him and wailed softly as her feet hit the floor.

"Poor little thing, so tired!" the woman said, standing up and folding the newspaper she'd been reading. "You're here, so we're open. We open early for the farmers, and it's nearly dawn. They'll be coming in soon."

"Yay!" Bell shouted. He scooted into the nearest booth.

"You folks just passing through?" the woman asked,

handing them menus as they crowded into the booth. Mattie and Maya and Tibby sat on one side, Bell and Da on the other. It was a really old-fashioned place, with jukeboxes on the wall at each booth. Mattie and Bell flipped through the lists of songs, looking for something they knew, but it was all country music from years and years ago.

"We broke down, just outside town," Maya said.

"Bad luck!" the woman exclaimed. "The garage opens around nine, if Jacko wants to work. Depends on the kind of night he's had."

Mattie opened the menu. Everything looked good to her. "Pancakes," she said. "Sausage. Juice."

"Me, too," Bell said.

"Me, too!" cried Tibby, waking fully. "Pancakes!" The mess she made with syrup could be epic, but Maya and Da were too tired to protest.

"Pancakes all around?" the woman asked, and Da nodded. "Coffee, please," he said. "Is it strong?"

"It'll wake you up," the woman promised. "I'm Audra, by the way. It's my place." The menus said *Audra's*, with a painted picture of the diner on them.

Audra went back to the kitchen, and cooking noises and good smells soon came wafting out. It wasn't long before she emerged again, first with steaming mugs of coffee and glasses of orange juice, and then with enormous plates of pancakes, butter melting on top, and a pitcher of real maple syrup, warmed, for the table.

"You folks on vacation?" Audra inquired as she passed the plates around. Mattie gulped orange juice thirstily. It didn't taste much like the juice she was used to. It tasted like real oranges. It was delicious.

Da and Maya exchanged glances. "Not exactly," Da said. "We're . . . performers."

"Artistes," Bell corrected him. It was what Maya always said.

"Oh, you're with the circus!" Audra exclaimed. "I should have guessed, the way you look."

Mattie glanced down at her jeans. What did she mean? Then she saw Audra smile at Maya, taking in her kohl-lined eyes and rose-colored sari, her rings and henna-painted hands and the silver bracelet that wrapped around her upper arm like a snake.

"We just put up the poster, see?" Audra pointed to a bulletin board near the door, and Mattie jumped up to look, Da following. There was a circus poster, all right. Gold and black and red, it showed a big top, a clown with a round red nose, and two tigers jumping through flaming hoops. Big gold letters announced *Master Morogh's Circus of Wonders*. Below were performance dates and times. It would open Thursday, in just five days, and run through Monday, Labor Day.

"It's been a long time since we had a circus here," Audra said. "My grandkids are wild to go. I have to admit, I'm pretty wild to go myself!"

Da stood behind Mattie, looking at the poster. Then he squeezed her shoulder and said to Audra, "Well, I guess we'll see you there, then!"

"Really?" Mattie said as they headed back to the table. "A circus? Really?"

"Could be," Da said, in a way that usually meant yes. Mattie felt a stir of excitement in her stomach. If she had to choose between a fair and a circus, she'd take a circus anytime. Circuses had other families, families of trapeze artists and animal trainers and tumblers. There weren't many circuses left, though, not the kind that would take on a whole family who did magic. They were either huge, three-ring deals or the kind that performed in fancy theaters with music and light shows. The Marvelwoods hadn't been with a circus since Mattie was seven years old.

"The circus is here through the long weekend," Da said to Maya when they sat down.

"What good timing for us!" Maya exclaimed.

"If it's the right kind," Da reminded her. "The poster makes it look small. It could suit us well, if they have a need for us."

"Yay, a circus! Clowns and elephants!" Bell said, and Tibby echoed, "Yay!" even though she didn't know what she was cheering for.

They sat back down and dug into the pancakes, and they were *good*. Tibby was head-to-toe syrup in no time, but not even Maya cared. They just ate and ate.

When everyone was done, they sat there groaning in a quiet, pleased way for a little while. The door opened, and a group of men came in—definitely the farmers Audra had mentioned, with their overalls and caps. The men ordered huge plates of eggs, ignoring the strangers sitting nearby, not even noticing Maya and her kohl-ringed sidelong glance. Audra had to hustle.

Da stood up to pay the bill and chatted with Audra by the cash register for a few minutes. Then he came back to the table.

"The circus is set up just the other side of town," he said. "Not too far."

"Ohhh," Mattie moaned. "I can't walk anymore!"

"All of us are tired, Mattie," Maya pointed out. "The sooner we get things settled, the sooner we can rest." Mattie scowled at her but scooted from the booth, and they headed out of the diner.

"See you Thursday!" Audra called as the door closed behind them.

The sun was up now, but it was still early. They walked by a clothing shop with a really pretty dress in the window, a hardware store, and a place that looked like it sold cards and books and a bunch of stuff that nobody really needed. Besides the diner, that was about it for the town. Then they passed a bank, and the sign in front read *Frog Creek Credit Union*.

"Is it Frog Creek, North Carolina?" Mattie asked. "Or did we get to South Carolina while I was asleep?"

"It's South Carolina," Da said. "We passed the border a while back."

Da had lifted an exhausted Tibby to his shoulders by the time they reached the dusty pasture where the circus was setting up. A high wooden fence surrounded it, and beyond the fence a forest of thick trees loomed. From this distance they could see the top of the big tent and hear the sounds of hammering and sawing and the occasional trumpet of an elephant. Mattie was glad: she really liked elephants, and not every small circus had them. They were a lot of trouble, Da always said, and expensive to feed.

The sun warmed Mattie's back as they came to the place where the welcome arch would be set up. In a few days, it would likely have a big banner with the circus name on it, and the ticket taker would sit just inside. Right now, though, it was just a gap in the fence. They stood together, gathering their strength for the introductions and conversations and explanations that would happen as soon as they stepped into the circus lot.

And then Mattie saw a man coming toward them. She could tell that he wasn't a roustabout—one of the circus workers—but some sort of artiste. He was short and kind of round, and Mattie noticed when he got close enough that he had unusual greenish-gray eyes with very high, arched brows. He wore pants with a gold stripe down the sides, a spotless white shirt with the sleeves rolled up, and black gloves. His hair, as shiny and black as his boots, was slicked back, and he had a funny little V-shaped beard that came to a sharp point.

Tibby bounced with excitement on Da's shoulders. "The ringmaster!" she squealed. "Are you the ringmaster?" She hadn't even been born the last time they'd been with a circus, but Da and Maya had told her stories about them, and Da had imaged up lions and tigers, clowns and acrobats and trapeze artists. She knew what a ringmaster would look like.

The man smiled and bowed as Da set Tibby down. "Hello, hello, hello!" he welcomed them in a low, rich voice with an accent like Da's. It was funny, Mattie thought, such a big voice coming from such a small person. "Yes, my dear, I am Master Morogh, owner and ringmaster."

And then Mattie's mouth dropped open in surprise as he said, "Welcome to my Circus of Wonders, Marvelwoods!"

CHAPTER 3

"**H**ow did he know our name?" Bell asked, breathless. He and Mattie almost had to jog to keep up as Master Morogh led the family across the tamped-down grass to the big top. The ringmaster was little, but he moved fast.

"Shh." Mattie was trying to hear what Da and Master Morogh were saying.

"But how did he *know*?" Bell insisted.

"Be quiet!" Mattie said.

"One of the rousties saw your truck broken down this morning," Master Morogh told Da. "We'll send someone out right away. We have some men who are good with engines. They'll get you up and running in no time."

"That would be grand," Da said, pleased.

"It must be fate!" Master Morogh clapped his hands together. "We needed some midway acts, and here you are. Perfect, perfect, perfect!" He bobbed his head up and down like a bird with each "perfect."

"He's weird, weird, weird," Bell whispered, and Mattie laughed, pulling Tibby along. Tibby floated just above the ground in protest at being yanked.

"Stay down!" Mattie told her, afraid the ringmaster would notice, and Tibby immediately became as heavy as lead. That was the other side of her ability, and it drove Mattie crazy. If she didn't want to be carried, or to go where she was supposed to go, she'd just get heavy. No one could move her then. "Tibby, please!" Mattie begged, and Tibby lightened up and walked again.

"So you're magicians?" Master Morogh said. "Rabbits out of hats, crystal balls and whatnot?"

"Something like that," Da replied.

Master Morogh came to an abrupt stop, turning, and Mattie nearly crashed into him. "And you, little girl—what do you do?"

"Me?" she said. "I . . . I read minds."

"Really!" He sounded impressed, but in that fake way grownups had when they really thought something was silly. "Would you like to read mine?"

He held out his gloved hand, and without thinking, Mattie laid hers over it. A little flash of static made her jump, but she couldn't read anything. Maybe it was the glove; she'd never tried anyone wearing one before.

"Oh—no," she stammered. "It takes . . . you know, some preparation."

"Of course," Master Morogh said. His eyes met hers sharply,

and his tone had changed a little. Mattie felt uncomfortable, though she couldn't have said why. "Silly of me. I know the routine. I have my own act, you know. I'm not just the ringmaster."

"What do you do?" Bell asked.

"I'm a hypnotist," he said. "Have you ever been hypnotized, my young friend?"

Mattie could see that he might be good at it. Those green eyes were compelling.

"You mean you put people to sleep?" Bell jumped with excitement. "Really? Could you do me?"

"Oh, surely, surely, surely!" Master Morogh exclaimed, his pointed beard bobbing. "When we're all squared away, you come see me. I'll be set up on the midway. We'll put you there, too, right across from me. It'll be marvelous, Marvelwoods!"

Tibby giggled. "Marvelous Marvelwoods. Marvelous Marvelwoods," she chanted, hopping on one foot.

"You're Scottish, aren't you?" Da asked Master Morogh as they started walking again. "I ken the accent, and the name. Though there aren't many Moroghs around anymore. That's an old name, that one." Mattie had never heard it before. She wasn't even sure if it was a first name or a last name.

"It was my own da's name," Master Morogh said. "And his da before him—the eldest of the family, for generations." A first name, then.

"And where do you hail from? What's your clan?"

Mattie knew that most Scots were from a clan, a group of people who were all related. Some clans were huge and had their own crests and their own patterns of plaid that were named after them. Her da was a Burnett, an old clan, but not as big and important as some. He'd taken his mother's name,

Marvelwood, because he thought it sounded better—more magical.

"I'm from way up north, a tiny little burgh in the Highlands. You'd never know it," Master Morogh said.

"Oh, I know them all," Da said. "My people are Travellers. I was one until I came over, twenty years ago. We went everywhere, doing our acts. I'm sure I've been through every village and down every wynd in Scotland."

"Really!" the ringmaster exclaimed. "Well, my people were innkeepers. We stayed put. Ah, here's my wagon now."

They had circled around behind the big tent to the back yard, where all the circus wagons were parked. Roustabouts ran to and fro, and Mattie breathed in the circus smells of dust and straw, popcorn and animals. It was so much better than the smell that fairs had, of motor oil and fried food and always, faintly, of vomit from people coming off the rides.

"Now, Mrs. Marvelwood—" Master Morogh looked at Mattie's mother.

"Maya," she said.

"Maya. Such a pretty name," he said. "Your husband and I will do some business, and you can go around and meet the other artistes. I'll send the boys for your truck."

Maya's eyebrows went up. "We do our business together, Simon and I," she said. "Mattie can mind the others while we talk."

"That is not my way," the ringmaster said.

This was the sort of thing that drove Maya wild. Mattie wondered if she'd protest. But no, this was a job, and they needed it.

"Very well," Maya said, her voice carefully controlled. "You are kind indeed to see to our truck. Come on, children."

Master Morogh and Da climbed the steps into the ringmaster's wagon, which was large and brightly painted gold and black, with a shiny red door. It had the circus's sign on it, the same sign from the flyer that hung in Audra's, and Mattie saw it painted on most of the other wagons and trucks parked nearby.

A smaller tent sat beyond the wagons. Smoke trailed out of a pipe at the top, carrying the smell of cooking meat. Mattie grabbed Bell's arm and pointed. "A cookhouse tent! Real food!"

"No more hotplate curries," Bell said, rubbing his hands together gleefully. There was no kitchen in their wagon, so Maya made one-pot meals on a hotplate when they were with a fair or circus that didn't have a cookhouse. Mattie and Bell both hated curries. The spiciness made their noses run.

"No more corn dogs!" Mattie cried, naming her least favorite food in the world. They tasted so disgusting. Even the name was disgusting. Bell loved them.

"Ooh, look," Tibby said, pointing, as one of the wagon doors opened and people began to pour out. A woman came down the stairs first, and then a man, and then a beautiful girl who looked almost grown up. All three were dark-haired and wiry and dressed in sparkly leotards and tights. The girl had a thick braid that came down to her hips. Behind her came two boys, one in tights and one in jeans. Last was another girl, short and thin, her head ringed with dark curls. She wore jeans and a T-shirt like Mattie, but her T-shirt had a unicorn made of shiny spangles on it.

They noticed Maya immediately, and the woman came over. "Well, hello!" she said. Her face was open and friendly, and Mattie liked her right away. "We're the Silvas. Aerialists. Are you an act? What do you do?"

"We are the Marvelwoods. We do magic, different kinds," Maya said. Her accent made her sound a little formal and standoffish, but that didn't seem to bother Mrs. Silva a bit.

"And you're joining on with us? That's fantastic!" she cried. "It'll be great to have another family around. I'm Sabella, and this is my husband Sebastian. This is my oldest son, Santos, and my daughter Sofia, and this one is Stefano, and my littlest, Selena." Sofia was gorgeous. She flashed the Marvelwoods a distracted smile as she examined her manicure. Santos, Stefano, and Selena looked almost exactly alike, except that Stefano and Selena were about a foot shorter and five or six years younger.

Mrs. Silva put out a hand to shake Maya's, but Maya clasped her hands behind her back and said, "My name is Maya. This is Tibby. Bell is my son; he is nine. And this is Mattie. She is eleven." Mattie followed Maya's lead and folded her own hands together. She and Maya didn't like shaking hands. It was usually no fun at all to know the futures or the thoughts of people they met.

"Welcome!" Mrs. Silva exclaimed. She seemed like a very enthusiastic person. "Selena is eleven, too. The girls can be friends. How wonderful!"

Mattie looked at the girl, Selena. She was staring at the ground, and her face had turned bright red, right up to the tips of her ears. It was nice to know that other people's mothers could be so embarrassing. But Mrs. Silva seemed really nice. She was sort of like a mother in a book, happy and friendly and funny.

Mattie decided to rescue Selena. "Hi," she said.

"Hi," Selena said back, still looking down.

"I like your shirt."

"Really?" Selena raised her head, her brown eyes shining. "I sewed it myself, with extra sequins. Can you tell it's a unicorn?"

"Definitely," Mattie assured her. "It's amazing. I can't sew at all."

Mattie could tell Selena was pleased. "Mom!" she said to Mrs. Silva. "Can I show Mattie around?"

"Oh, can I go, Maya?" Mattie pleaded.

Mrs. Silva looked at Maya, who shrugged. "Go ahead, girls," Mrs. Silva replied. "Just stay out of the rousties' way. And keep away from those tigers."

"Really, tigers?" Mattie said, wide eyed. "I've never been at a circus with tigers before."

"Master Morogh brought them," Selena told her. "Them and Ahmad, their trainer. I think they're kind of scary."

"The tigers or the trainer?"

"Both," Selena said, grinning. "Come on, let's go see the Bellamys!" She grabbed Mattie's hand, pulling her forward.

At the touch, Selena's thoughts bounced around in Mattie's head. *Yay, a girl my age!* she heard. *At last, at last, at last! So much fun!* Mattie had been thinking the exact same thing. She smiled back at Selena and wriggled her hand free, hoping Selena wouldn't notice and take offense. It was nice to know that Selena was glad she was there, but it seemed kind of creepy to keep on reading her.

"That was your mother, right? You call her Maya?" Selena asked as they walked among the wagons.

Mattie explained. "When I was little, I kept getting *mama* and *Maya* mixed up, so I just ended up calling her Maya. Besides, she's not really the mama type."

"Boy, if I called my mother Sabella . . ." Selena bared her

teeth to show how angry her mother would be, but then she laughed. Mattie couldn't see that kind-looking woman getting too mad about anything.

"So what do you do, Mattie? In your act, I mean?"

"I read minds," Mattie said.

"Oh, I would *love* to do that!" Selena cried. "Wouldn't it be brilliant if it was real? You'd always know if a boy liked you, or why someone was mad at you."

"Maybe," Mattie said. "Well, maybe not. Think of the things you wouldn't want to know."

Selena stopped walking. "That's true. It could be bad, right?" She bit her lip. "It could be horrible. What if your best friend really hated you? Or your sister thought you were hideously ugly?"

"Exactly." Mattie was pleased that Selena understood.

"But on the other hand, what if you found out something bad that you could do something about? Like if someone was in trouble?"

"What could you do, though?" Mattie asked. This had happened to her once. A boy she'd read had a stepfather who beat him. Not just spankings or slaps, but real beatings with a belt. It was awful. She had seen it as clear as anything, but what could she say? She never told anyone, not even Da, though she'd always thought she should have. But Da would have said something, or confronted the boy's parents. And then what? Either they wouldn't have believed that she really knew and there would have been a fight, or they would have believed, and . . . well, it just couldn't happen. She still felt horrible about it.

"Hmm." Selena started walking again. Mattie admired the way she moved; she was graceful, almost like she was dancing.

Her toes pointed out, and her back was perfectly straight. Mattie tried to straighten up herself.

"So you do the trapeze stuff?" Mattie asked.

"Some of it. The less dangerous moves," Selena replied.

"Isn't it scary?"

"I love it," she said. "It's like flying. There's a moment when you let go of the bar and you're just in the air. Sometimes I think if I flap my arms, I'll keep going, like a bird."

They came to a big wagon with a sign on the side that read *The Remarkable Bellamy Brothers*. "I hope they're in there," Selena said. "They can't be practicing because it's our time, but they might've gone into town."

"Who are they?" Mattie asked.

"They're acrobats, tumblers," Selena said. "They're really nice."

She was about to knock on the wagon door when Mattie held up her hand. "Wait. What's that?" A low rumble seemed almost to shake the ground. It went on and on.

Selena listened. "That's the tigers," she said with a little shiver.

"Can we see them? Just for a second?" Mattie pleaded.

"Well . . . okay. Then we'll come back."

Mattie followed Selena around the Bellamys' wagon to the wagon parked in front of it. All sorts of animals were painted on the sides in colors so bright they almost hurt to look at— lions, bears, and wolves, all with long, sharp, white teeth. The front of the wagon had bars like a jail cell, and behind the bars were the tigers.

The girls stood very still, and Mattie looked at the tigers. They were light orange with black stripes, like tigers in pictures, but a little smaller than she had expected. Not that they were actually small; she thought that if they stood on their hind legs, they'd probably be way taller than Da. One of them paced back and forth in the wagon, its muscles rippling as it moved. It had to turn and go the other way every couple of steps because there was so little room. The other one lay in the front, looking out. It had pushed one of its paws between the bars, and the paw swayed a little, like it was waving.

"They're beautiful," Mattie breathed.

"Yeah," Selena agreed. "They really are. I'm glad they're in a cage, though. One's a girl and one's a boy. Ahmad calls them Hasha and Hadi."

"Hasha," Mattie whispered to the one lying down. "Hasha, hello." She moved a little closer.

"Mattie, watch out," Selena warned nervously.

"It's okay," Mattie assured her. "I just want to see her eyes."

Hasha stared right at Mattie. The tiger's eyes were amber, and Mattie could see herself reflected in them. She could see something else there, too, but she wasn't sure what. Was it sadness? She didn't know what sadness would look like in a tiger. It was completely different from looking into a person's eyes, but for some reason, she wasn't a bit afraid. She moved closer, and closer still. Selena let out a little squeak, but Mattie barely heard it.

And then she reached out and put her hand over Hasha's huge, sharp-clawed paw.

CHAPTER 4

Right away, behind her closed eyes, Mattie got a rush of images. A jungle, it looked like, with the most amazing trees and vines winding around them from the floor of the forest, up and up. Flowers and leaves so thick that the sun's rays couldn't get through, so the light was all murky and green. Little quick visions, like short movies, of animals—lizards and snakes and some ratty-looking thing she'd never seen before twisting and dodging through the underbrush. Sounds, even—weird birdcalls and something else shrieking.

And on top of all that was the feeling. Sad, it was so sad, but not like any sorrow she'd ever known. It was grief so deep and raw that it hurt, and Mattie had to clutch herself like she'd been hit in the stomach. There weren't any words, just the images and the terrible, mournful feeling.

And then she was tumbling backward, hitting the dusty ground hard, the breath knocked out of her. For a second she wasn't sure what had happened. Had the tiger swiped at her?

"What do you think you are doing?" a furious voice asked. Mattie struggled to breathe, gasping and wheezing, until she could inhale. A man loomed over her. He wore a white robe over leggings, and a turban covered his hair. Uh-oh. The tamer.

"I'm sorry," Mattie said in a small voice. "I just . . . I didn't . . ." She put a tentative hand up to her face, where she could feel wetness. Blood? But no, when she looked at her hand she didn't see any red. The wetness wasn't blood, it was tears. The tiger had made her cry.

"Get out of here, girl, and do not let me see you around my tigers again," the man snarled.

Selena helped Mattie to her feet. "You didn't have to knock her down, Ahmad!"

The man scowled. "They are not pets, Selena. They could have bitten her hand right off. I had to get her away from them quickly."

"I'm sorry," Mattie said again. "It was stupid."

"It was incredibly stupid," Ahmad agreed. "You are lucky still to be in one piece." As the girls walked away, he stood watching them, making sure they went.

As soon as they were out of sight, Selena stopped and turned to Mattie. "What the heck *was* that?" she demanded.

"Um . . . what do you mean?" Mattie asked, though she was pretty sure what Selena meant.

"You touched that tiger—I can't believe you did that!— and then you said, 'I'm so sorry, I'm so sorry.' And you got all weird. And the tiger got all weird, too."

"Weird?" Mattie repeated, stalling for time.

"Your eyes were closed. You looked like you were in some kind of trance, but you were crying. And the tiger almost looked like it was crying, too."

"It did?"

"What were you sorry about? It was like you were talking to her."

Mattie clenched her teeth. She couldn't tell. She *couldn't*. "I don't know. I was just . . . pretending."

Selena raised her eyebrows. "Well, if you don't want to tell me, that's your business."

She started to walk away, and Mattie panicked. This was the first chance at a friend she'd had in years. She knew she'd get in trouble for it, but she couldn't just let Selena go.

"Wait," Mattie said in a low voice. Selena stopped but didn't turn. "You're right. It's something weird."

Selena spun around. "I knew it!" she said triumphantly. "Well, what? Are you really a tiger tamer, too? Or part tiger yourself? How weird *is* it?"

Mattie had to smile. "Not *that* weird," she said, and took a deep breath. "It's just . . . just that I can sort of read minds. I mean, really read them."

Selena narrowed her eyes. "What do you mean?"

Mattie shrugged, trying to seem casual. "What I said. I can read minds."

"Like . . . what people think?"

"And animals, too, I guess. I'd never done that before. Just cats and dogs, and they don't really think much."

"They don't? Even cats? But they always . . . wait. You can really *read minds*?" Selena put a hand over her mouth. Mattie could see her thoughts going wild, even though she couldn't read them. Selena had the kind of face that showed everything. It showed that she was wondering what she'd thought in the last hour, what Mattie might have read.

"I have to be touching the person," Mattie told her. "Or tiger. It's okay. You didn't think anything bad."

"Okay," Selena said, a little doubtfully. "But—what was the tiger thinking?"

Mattie closed her eyes, remembering. "She was so unhappy. I think she misses her home, wherever that is. I couldn't tell. It was a forest somewhere. She was just really, really sad."

"How awful." Selena frowned. "I've never thought about how the tigers felt. That cage is so small. They must hate it."

Mattie nodded.

"Wow," Selena said quietly. "You can really read minds. That's amazing. Isn't it?"

"Sort of," Mattie said. "Sometimes. Sometimes it's horrible."

"But it's a secret? Why? You'd be really famous if people knew. You'd be on television and everything!"

"It's the *and everything* part that's a problem." Mattie tried to think of the best way to explain it. "Think about it. People would go nuts. Everybody in the world would want to know what their friends or their husbands or their parents or their kids thought."

Selena shuddered. "Oh boy, if my mother knew what I thought . . ."

"And maybe the police or something would want to know what suspects or criminals thought. And then the CIA would want to know what spies thought. I'd end up spending all my time reading nasty spies who'd tortured and killed people."

Selena looked both horrified and fascinated.

"Or else maybe they'd want to study me. The government, I mean. So they could figure out how it works and give it to other people. Only—how would they study me? They'd have to put me in some awful room and hook things up to my brain and give me tests all the time. Or take it out."

"Take what out?"

"My brain."

Selena let out a little *eep*. "No, that's crazy! They wouldn't take out your brain!"

"Well, that's the kind of thing I think about," Mattie said. She didn't tell Selena that was the kind of thing her parents talked about sometimes, when they thought the kids weren't listening. It had been drummed into them since they were old enough to understand that no one must ever know.

And now she'd told Selena.

"What about the rest of your family?" Selena asked. "Your wagon says you read minds, and you really do. Do they do real stuff, too?"

Mattie gulped. She wasn't prepared for this. "Oh—no, of course not!" she said. "It's just me. I'm like—a mutant or something. Their acts are just ordinary." It felt wrong, somehow, to lie to Selena, but she had to. It was bad enough that she'd told about her own talent.

Selena was quiet for a minute.

"I'm glad you told me," she said finally. "I won't tell anyone else, I promise. But . . . I've never had a friend who could read my mind before. It's going to take some getting used to."

"I understand," Mattie said. Selena would think about it, and then she'd decide it was just too strange. And Mattie *did* understand. She wouldn't want a friend knowing everything she thought either. She turned away, hunching her shoulders as protection against Selena's *okay, see you later* that she knew would actually mean *see you never.*

"Where are you going?" Selena asked.

"Back to the rest of the freak family," Mattie said. Then she stopped, her hand to her mouth. Now Selena would know Mattie had lied about her family and their talents.

But Selena didn't notice. "Don't call yourself that! You are not a freak!"

"No?" Mattie said. "How does that work, being a mind reader but not a freak?"

Selena stamped her foot, and a little puff of dust rose up from the dry ground. "It's a *gift*. Even if it's one you don't much like. It's like being great at art, or singing. Or like being a math genius. It doesn't make you a freak." She paused, thinking. "Or if it does, you're a freak in a good way. Like, special. Unique."

Mattie had heard this a hundred times from Maya, but it sounded different coming from Selena. It sounded almost believable.

Then Selena grinned. "And you did say you'd visit the Bellamys with me."

It was a minute before what she said registered. "You still want me to? Really?" Mattie asked.

"Yes, really. C'mon, Mattie!" Selena held out a hand, then snatched it back, remembering that Mattie could read her mind with a touch. For a moment they were both embarrassed, but then Selena laughed, and, relieved, Mattie laughed, too.

They wound their way past another few wagons until they were back at the Bellamys'. The door was open now, and Selena poked her head in.

"Bellamys!" she shouted. "Come out and meet someone new!"

A crash came from inside. Then a man jumped down the wagon steps, short, kind of squat, muscled all over. He had a buzz cut and a handlebar mustache, and wore tight stretchy pants and a sleeveless tee.

Another Bellamy jumped out. Mattie blinked. He looked exactly like the first. *Exactly.* Same mustache, same outfit, same face. Then a third, just like the others. A fourth. A fifth. Mattie knew her mouth was hanging open, and Selena burst into laughter.

"They're quintuplets!" she cried. "All identical. But I can tell them apart."

"She can," one of the quintuplets said. "We don't know how she does it."

Selena pointed to one Bellamy. "This is Elso. This one is Maso. He's Harma. That one's Negyed. And he's Oto."

"She got it right again!" one of the Bellamys crowed.

"Hi," Mattie said, a little faintly.

"And this is Mattie," Selena said. "Her family's joining us. They're magicians."

"Excellent!" a Bellamy—Elso?—said. "Always nice to have new folk."

"Their names mean First, Second, Third, Fourth, and Fifth," Selena told Mattie. "In Hungarian, I think."

"Our mom's Hungarian," a Bellamy explained. "It was easier for her that way. She didn't have to remember actual names. Five's a lot of kids, especially all at once. And especially when they all look the same."

"I can imagine," Mattie said, gazing at them. It was like being in a funhouse room with mirrors, the same person reflected over and over.

"Hey, guys, show her what you can do," Selena urged.

The Bellamys exchanged glances, and then without any warning, one of them gave a little hop and went sailing through the air and landed on the shoulders of two others. A fourth climbed up the two at the bottom and the one on their shoulders as if they were a tree, and then he was standing on the top one's shoulders. The fifth one shook his head and said, "I'm a little tired today."

A moment later the two on top jumped down, did somersaults, and sprang back to their feet, and all four bowed. Mattie and Selena clapped, and Mattie exclaimed, "You're amazing!"

"Except for Oto," his brother said. "He's just lazy."

Oto sighed and then bent over backward, put his hands on the ground, flipped, and continued flipping backward in a circle until he was back where he'd started. Mattie applauded wildly.

"Show-off," a brother muttered.

"You're all really good," Mattie assured them. "I can't wait to see your act!"

"We'll be rehearsing in a couple of hours. You should come by and watch," Oto suggested. His brothers nodded.

"If I can," Mattie promised.

"Rehearsing—uh-oh, I'm late," Selena said. "Come on!"

The girls waved to the quintuplets and started back to the big top. "Nice to meet you," Mattie called back to them, watching as they leaped up the steps into their wagon. Their legs were like springs.

Selena was hurrying, and Mattie jogged along beside her. "They look exactly the same," Mattie said, amazed. She'd seen twins before, but nothing more than that.

"Well, they're identical," Selena pointed out. "But actually, there's something just a tiny bit different about each of them."

"Really? What?"

Selena giggled. "You'll have to figure it out for yourself," she said. "I have to practice now. Want to watch?"

"There's our wagon," Mattie said, pointing. A truck had pulled up in front of the tent, in the area where the midway would be, and hooked onto it was the Marvelwoods' wagon. "I should find my mother. I'll come later, okay?"

"Okay—see you!" Selena ran into the big top.

The wagon door was open, and Mattie stuck her head in. Maya sat in the lotus position on one of the carpets in the center of the main room, breathing deeply. Her hands rested on her knees, each thumb and forefinger making a little *o*. Her eyes were closed.

"Where's Da?" Mattie asked.

"I am meditating," Maya said pointedly without opening her eyes. It was one of the major rules of the family: Don't interrupt Maya while she's meditating. The only more important rule was *don't tell anyone that what we do is real*. And Mattie had just broken that one. She caught her breath when she thought about it. She couldn't believe she'd told Selena, and suddenly she was afraid Maya would see it in her face if she looked up.

"Sorry," Mattie said, and backed out again.

She didn't see Da or Bell anywhere, so she ducked into the big top. It was a single-ring tent. The bleachers weren't set up yet, so it seemed strangely empty. The ring had been assembled, though, and Bell and Tibby were standing with some other people at the edge, watching the Silvas practice. Master Morogh stood off to the side by himself, his face turned upward. Mattie made her way over to Bell.

"Da's off fixing the truck with some of the roustics," Bell said. "I've been hanging out with Stefano. That's him." He pointed to the younger of the two boys they'd met earlier, who was climbing down the ladder from the trapeze platform.

"Mattie, look!" Tibby cried. "They're on the trapezes!"

Mattie looked up just as Santos let go of his sister Sofia's hand. Sofia went sailing through the air in a beautiful arc, and her father, Sebastian, caught her easily as he swung toward her on the catch bar. They were so graceful that it wasn't even scary to watch. There didn't seem to be any doubt that Mr. Silva would catch Sofia, or that Santos would reach out from his trapeze and grab her feet as she swung back in the other direction.

"Wow," Mattie said, impressed.

"Wow!" Tibby repeated. "I want to try!" Mattie grinned, imagining Tibby sailing past Mr. Silva's outstretched arms and up to the top of the tent.

"You don't need a trapeze," Mattie pointed out. Pleased, Tibby started to rise, but Mattie pushed her down. "Remember, you're supposed to stay on the ground around people," she warned in a low voice. Another rule. But Tibby couldn't be blamed for breaking it—she was only four.

Sofia practiced her specialties next. First she performed on the aerial hoop, which looked just like a hanging hula hoop. Mattie had never seen anyone on the hoop before. Sofia sat on it and swung to and fro like it was a regular swing, then twirled through it, spun around, weaved her body up over and under it. It was like ballet in the air. After that she did a hair hang, where she swung suspended by her long braid. It looked like it must have hurt, but Sofia smiled and smiled through it. Like the other Silvas, she had an amazing smile, so wide and bright that you could see it from far below. Even hanging from her hair way up high, she was beautiful.

"How does she do that?" Mattie asked Tibby, and Tibby pulled her own short reddish-blond hair hard and said, "Ouch!"

48

Then it was Selena's turn. She sprang up the rungs as quick and sure as a cat. As Sofia swung up onto the board, done with her practice moves, Selena grabbed her fly bar and sailed off the platform. Mattie held her breath. Selena swung out and back, out and back, doing a force back with her legs to push herself higher and higher. And then, as she swung toward her father, she let go of the trapeze and somersaulted through the air. She stretched her arms out, and Mr. Silva reached out and caught her easily. It was beautiful to watch.

When the Silvas were finished, the rousties placed a tightrope above the net, and a tall, slender woman with dark skin and cropped hair climbed the ladder to a lower platform. She wore a spangled red tutu and red slippers and carried a red and blue striped parasol. She moved with ease and confidence, almost skipping over the tightrope and doing intricate dance steps with her parasol as her partner.

"Who's that?" Mattie asked Selena and Sofia, who had joined them. The Bellamys had come in, too, and stood to the side, watching.

"It's Julietta. Julietta the Canary-Voiced Funambulist," Selena replied, making the title sound as if she were announcing it.

"Is she fun?" Tibby asked.

Selena giggled. "Well, yes, she is. But a funambulist is a tightrope walker."

"Funam. Funum. Fumbalist," Tibby tried.

"Oh, listen!" Selena said. Above them, Julietta had stopped in the middle of the rope. She opened her mouth and began to sing. The song wasn't in English; Mattie had no idea what language it was. She could barely tell that there was a tune, either. *Canary-voiced* was a real exaggeration.

"She's not such a great singer," Bell whispered to Mattie.

Selena and Sofia exchanged a look. "I don't know what's wrong with her," Selena said. "Usually, she sounds amazing. I hope she's not getting sick!"

Julietta cleared her throat and started again, but her voice was even worse this time, hoarse and breaking. She coughed and wobbled on the wire. The third try was the worst. Mattie thought she sounded like a crow choking on a piece of roadkill.

The tightrope walker didn't even try to get back to her platform. She jumped off the rope, landing with a graceful bounce on the net below. Then she scrambled to the edge and dropped to the ground.

Sofia ran over to her, the others following behind.

"What's wrong? Are you sick?" Sofia asked. "Let's get you some tea with honey."

"I'm not sick," Julietta replied. Her forehead was creased with frustration. "I don't think I am, anyway. I just can't . . . I can't sing."

"A singing funambulist who can't sing?" It was Master Morogh. Mattie hadn't noticed that he'd joined the little group huddled around Julietta. His triangular brows were drawn together, and he didn't look pleased at all.

"Try it again, Julietta," he commanded.

Once more Julietta climbed up the ladder and pranced across the tightrope, twirling her parasol. Midway across, she opened her mouth to sing. Only a hoarse screech came out. Mattie winced.

"Come down, my dear," Master Morogh said. His voice was gentle, but Julietta cringed at his words. She wobbled across the rope and made her way down the ladder to stand in front of the ringmaster. She seemed shrunken, almost as short as he was.

"So," Master Morogh said. "Your lovely voice is gone. That is a terrible, terrible, terrible shame."

"I don't know why," Julietta said in a husky whisper. "I'm sure it's only temporary."

"We cannot count on that, can we? What if it never returns? Without it, you're of no use to the Circus of Wonders. No use at all!"

Julietta gasped. "Are you firing me?" she asked. "I'll be fine by tomorrow. I know I will!"

"But we are a small circus." Master Morogh's tone was sympathetic. "We cannot afford to keep on performers who don't perform. And what good is a canary-voiced funambulist without the voice of a canary?"

Julietta drew in a long, shaky breath. "No," she protested. "Please—"

"I must let you go, my dear. I'm sorry. Very, very, very sorry indeed. I am sure you can find work elsewhere, with your talent on the wire. But you are no longer needed here."

Master Morogh crossed his arms over his chest, waiting. Mattie and Selena and the Bellamys stared at him, then turned to Julietta. Tears ran down her cheeks as she wept in silence.

"Now, wait a minute—," one of the Bellamys began. Master Morogh turned to him. Whatever the Bellamy saw in the ringmaster's face silenced him.

"Oh, Julietta!" Sofia cried. She ran to the tightrope walker and hugged her hard. "I'll get my mom. Maybe she has some medicine . . ."

"She can't help," Julietta said shakily. "Without my voice, I'm no good here." She squeezed Sofia and Selena tightly and gave each Bellamy a hug. To Mattie she said, "I'm sorry we didn't get a chance to know each other. Maybe another time."

The ringmaster watched the farewells with a look of deep concern. But as Julietta stumbled out, Sofia's arm around her, Mattie glanced again at Master Morogh and noticed that he slowly rubbed his gloved hands together as his gaze followed them out of the tent.

CHAPTER 5

Mattie and the others walked back to the wagons in the hot sun.

"At least I managed the somersault," Selena said.

"You were amazing!" Mattie said. "I can barely do a somersault on the ground!"

"That's true," Bell agreed. "You're really clumsy." Tibby giggled, and Mattie reached out to poke him.

"Anyone can improve." They spun around. It was Master Morogh again. How had he sneaked up behind them?

The ringmaster smiled, and his little V-shaped beard bobbed. "You must try to improve all the time. Practice, practice, practice!" He reached out to pat Selena on the shoulder, but she ducked, scowling, as he walked off.

"He's so creepy," Selena whispered. "He's always every-where you don't want him to be. He sees everything."

"He says everything nine times!" Tibby said, pleased. Nine was her favorite number.

Mattie gazed after Master Morogh. There was something about him—his beard and his black gloves and his repeating—that really was kind of creepy. Mattie didn't like him, though she couldn't say why.

One of the Bellamys spoke. "That's just cruel, what he did to Julietta. We're all together here. We help each other."

"Master Morogh doesn't," Mattie said.

"No, he doesn't," another Bellamy agreed. "He likes to fire people. He's done that a lot."

"That's right," Selena said. "I remember hearing about . . . who was it? Oh, the sword swallower!"

"Yes," a third Bellamy said. "We were here then. Morogh tossed him right out."

"Why?"

"Well, he couldn't swallow the swords anymore. Imagine that."

Mattie winced. "Ouch," she said, and the Bellamy nodded.

"Exactly. He nearly cut his own head right off."

"Did that really happen, Maso?" Selena asked. She sounded uncertain.

"Is anything in a circus real?" Maso asked. "Are you real? Am I?" He flipped backward in a circle, breaking the solemn spell that Julietta's firing had cast.

Mattie stared at Maso, her eyes narrowed. It was impossible to tell if he was just fooling around or trying to say something serious.

"Good-bye, all!" The other Bellamys followed their brother, backflipping in a line toward their wagon.

"Poor Julietta," Selena said as she walked Mattie, Bell, and Tibby to their door. "I hope she can find another job."

"I'll bet she can," Mattie said. "She's really good on the tightrope—as long as she doesn't sing."

Selena nodded morosely. "I guess we'd all better watch out. I mean, if I fall on the trapeze, is he going to fire me?"

Mattie snorted. "Will he fire your clowns if their red noses come off? Will he fire the elephant if it poops in the ring?"

"Mattie!" Selena couldn't help smiling, and Tibby hooted with laughter.

"He's going to hypnotize me," Bell told Selena. "He said he would."

"You shouldn't," Selena said. Mattie looked at her sharply.

"Why not?" Bell asked.

Selena scuffed the dirt with her soft slipper. "You just shouldn't. I've seen him do it. It's . . ." Her voice trailed off.

"Creepy?" Mattie offered.

"Worse than creepy."

Bell frowned. "Well, I want to get hypnotized, and I'm going to."

"Watch his act on opening night," Selena advised. "Then decide."

There was lunch after rehearsals, in the big cookhouse tent. Maya came, and the Marvelwoods sat with the Silvas. The tent had three long picnic tables, and the muscled, blue-jeaned rousties talked and laughed with the artistes, who wore spandex and sequins. At some circuses, Mattie knew, the groups ate apart. There were plenty of artistes who thought they were better than the rousties and wouldn't spend time with them. Mattie was pleased to see that at the Circus of Wonders, everyone sat together.

"Master Morogh eats in his wagon," Selena said as Mattie looked around. "Thank goodness."

People stopped by to greet them. They met the cook, Stewie, and Selena introduced Maya to the Bellamys and got all their names right again. Tibby's face when the quintuplets came up to her was priceless. For once, she was too amazed to say a word. But as soon as they left to get their own lunch trays, she exploded.

"Nine of them! All the same!"

Everyone laughed, which annoyed her.

"Five," Mattie corrected, but Tibby shook her head.

"Nine, all just the same!" she said in a hushed voice. Nine it was, then.

Ahmad the tiger tamer was already eating when they sat down, and he didn't bother to get up and come over. He didn't even look their way. Mattie was secretly glad, fearful that he might say something about the incident with his cats. But Dee the bullhand, who trained both the elephants and the dogs, plopped her tray down next to Mrs. Silva.

"You do dogs and elephants both?" Mattie asked, taking a bite of macaroni and cheese. It was delicious.

"Don't speak with your mouth full," Maya scolded automatically.

Mattie frowned. "Stop nagging!" she hissed.

Dee ran her hands through her short blond hair, making it stand straight up. There was a streak of bright blue that ran down the back of her head, and she had seven earrings in one ear and four in the other. Tattoos covered her arms—not snakes, like Dane at the carnival, but vivid vines and flowers and small, strange birds.

"Pinga—that's the elephant—she's old," she said. "She was

56

already trained when we got her. She's been in the circus since she was born, and her parents before her. And the dogs—well, I just love dogs. And the dogs love Pinga. So we all work together."

"The dogs love the elephant?" Bell asked, intrigued.

Dee laughed. "Really, they do. You have to see it. They're all in the act. They sleep together at night."

This idea excited Tibby so much she almost floated off the bench. Mattie grabbed her. "We'll go look after lunch if you stay put," she promised in a whisper, pushing Tibby back down.

Bell was just lifting an apple to his mouth to take a bite when someone reached from behind and grabbed it out of his hand. The Marvelwoods spun around to see an immensely tall, skinny man with streaks of white makeup on his face throw the apple in the air. A second person—a man in a big red clown nose—caught it, and suddenly he was juggling two apples. A third, wearing oversized pants and with a bird perched on his shoulder, tossed in an orange, which matched the color of his frizzy hair, and now three objects spun, red–orange–red, almost too fast to see. Tibby howled with delight until the juggler caught the fruit, then bowed low to the Marvelwoods' applause. The three men sat down on the other side of the table.

"I'm Solomon," the juggler said. "This oaf here is Bub, and the nut with the bird is Chaz. We're clowns."

At first Mattie thought that the gray parrot on Chaz's shoulder was fake—it sat so still and looked so elegant—but when Bub grabbed Chaz's mac and cheese, the bird squawked, "Thief! Thief!" Chaz reached over and got Bub in a headlock, but Bub flipped Chaz over his shoulder, rattling the table, spilling drinks, and making the bird flutter to another table where it shrieked, "Stop that, gentlemen! Stop that!" Tibby laughed so hard Mattie was afraid she'd wet her pants.

After lunch, the Marvelwoods all took a nap in the wagon to make up for the nearly sleepless night. It was almost dusk when Mattie got up, groggy with that awful post-nap feeling. But when Maya answered a soft knock at the door, Tibby's shriek of joy roused her fast. She scrambled out of her bunk and ran into the main room.

Tibby stood gazing up, up, up at an enormous elephant right outside the wagon. Dee had her hand on the beast's leg. The elephant was old; it was obvious from her bleary eyes. She'd seen a lot. Mattie was tempted to touch her, but recalling the desolation of Hasha's thoughts, she held back.

"Oooh," Tibby breathed, awed. She'd never seen a real elephant before—only the ones Da conjured up. She reached out, but Dee stopped her.

"You have to be really careful, Tibby," Dee warned. "She's gentle, but she doesn't like surprises. Let her know you're there."

"Hello," Tibby whispered.

"She's a little deaf," Dee said.

"Hello!" Tibby shouted. The elephant blinked. Her eyes were nearly hidden in wrinkled gray skin. Tibby held out her hand, and the elephant curled her trunk and then uncurled it, touching Tibby's hand. At the end of the trunk was a sort of finger, and it stroked Tibby's palm.

"It's warm," Tibby said, amazed.

"That's Pinga's way of saying hi," Dee told her. "It's like she's shaking hands." Bell shook hands with the elephant next, and then Mattie held out her hand, forgetting.

Tired. Sleep, sleep. A wash of images, like with the tiger: bumping along in a wagon, circus rings. Loud music. Dogs barking. A feeling of contentment and drowsiness.

Mattie took her hand away and yawned so wide it hurt her jaw. Dee laughed. "You're as sleepy as she is!"

"Poor old thing," Mattie said. "It must be her bedtime."

"She just had her rehearsal. A little hay for her, then rest. Come on and meet the dogs."

"Can we?" Mattie asked Da. Da nodded his approval, and they ran off with Dee to the elephant's wagon. Four dogs napped in the straw there, but they woke up in a hurry when they noticed new people. A white, fuzzy one started licking Tibby's face the minute it saw her. A wiry terrier type jumped as high as Mattie's shoulder. A little hairless pup that looked kind of ratlike ran in circles, yapping wildly. The fourth was black and white, bigger than the others, with spots on his paws like little polka-dotted socks. He trotted right up to Mattie and sat at her feet, cocking his head to one side.

"That's Tray," Dee said. "The other ones are Blanch, Sweetheart, and Crab. Tray is the boss. He's really smart."

"Hey, Tray," Mattie said, petting him. *Treat, food?* she heard. *Walk?* This was what she usually got from dogs. From cats it was just food and petting and sometimes *Leave me alone.* But then, as Mattie stroked Tray's soft ears, she heard, *Different from the others.* Was he thinking that about her? Mattie stared at him, and he cocked his head to the other side. He looked like he was smiling.

The other dogs leaped around her, and their minds were full of *play* and *snack.* Tibby sat right down among them and they crawled all over her, except for Tray, who stayed by Mattie's side.

"Looks like you have a friend," Dee said. She tossed Mattie a dog biscuit, and Mattie handed it to Tray.

"He's wonderful." Mattie scratched him behind his ears. *Oooh, nice,* he thought. *Good human.* She laughed.

"All right, kids," Dee said to the dogs. "Bedtime."

Obediently, the dogs followed Pinga as she made her way heavily into her wagon, and they curled up in the straw around her stumpy feet. "She sleeps standing up," Dee explained. "Otherwise, she'd never get back up."

"Good night, dogs and elephant!" Tibby called to them. "See you tomorrow!"

They joined the others in the tent for dinner, a delicious meal of thick stew and hot biscuits and pie, and then the rousties built a bonfire in the field behind the big top. There were three of them who were permanent with the circus— Juan, Sal, and Max—all in jeans and dirty tees. They'd made friends with Da already, since they'd fixed the truck together, and Da helped them drag tree branches over to the fire. Bell, Tibby, and Mattie roasted marshmallows over the flames, and Selena and her brother Stefano came over to sit with them.

Selena plopped down next to Maya, who sat cross-legged on a blanket. "What's that on your hand?" she asked.

Maya held out her hand, which was covered with henna designs of flowers and leaves.

"Wow," Selena said, awed. "That is so pretty!"

Mattie looked at the tracery. She didn't usually notice it, but it *was* kind of pretty. Maya did the henna work herself. She always urged Mattie to try it out, but Mattie refused.

"Would you like me to paint some on you?" Maya asked Selena, giving Mattie a sideways look. Mattie rolled her eyes.

"Really, would you? I'd love it!" Selena said.

Maya smiled a real smile, not one of her dreamy fortune-teller smiles. "Come by when you have some free time," she said, and Selena clapped her hands with pleasure.

Sal the roustie brought out a mandolin. He sang in a rough, low voice traveling songs Mattie had never heard before. Then Da conferred with him and they sang a Scottish tune together in perfect harmony.

> For fame and for fortune I wandered the earth
> And now I've come back to the land of my birth
> I've brought back my treasures but only to find
> They're less than the pleasures I first left behind
>
> For these are my mountains and this is my glen
> The braes of my childhood will know me again
> No land's ever claimed me tho' far I did roam
> For these are my mountains and I'm going home.

It was a mournful tune. Mattie gazed at the faces around the fire, all a little sad but in a good way, the kind of sadness that music can make you feel.

They sang a livelier song next, with one of the rousties keeping time with sticks on a log, a homemade drum, and everyone joining in for the chorus. Before long, Solomon had grabbed Mrs. Silva for a dance, and then Da did a jig while Sal played and they all clapped in time to the beat of the stick-drum. Da was wild in the firelight, his face as red as his hair as he danced.

"Your dad is Scottish, right?" Selena asked, swaying to the music. Mattie nodded. "And your mom is . . . ?"

"Indian," Mattie said. "India Indian."

"How'd they meet?"

"In California. They were part of a circus there for a while. They're both from Traveller families, but Maya's people came from India to Ireland and then went to California. She was born there."

"Travellers? You mean they like to travel?"

Mattie shook her head. "No. Well, yes, but that's not what it means. Travellers are people who move around from place to place, like artistes do. Lots of them are artistes, but some of them just live that way, doing odd jobs and stuff. They're sort of nomads, but in Scotland or Ireland, not in the desert."

"Huh," Selena said. "That is so much more interesting than my family. We're all from Florida. Just plain Florida. So your parents are like Gypsies?"

"No," Mattie told her. "Gypsies are from different places than Travellers. And lots of people use *Gypsy* almost like a bad word. People don't like Gypsies. They think they steal and give people the evil eye. It's not true, but we still don't like to be called that."

"Sorry!" Selena said, holding up her hands. "I'll never say it again."

There was a sudden silence, and Mattie looked up as Master Morogh walked into the flickering firelight. He'd taken off his fancy jacket but still wore his ringmaster's pants and shirt and his black gloves. He signaled to the musicians, opened his mouth, and began to sing.

Though Master Morogh's speaking voice was deep and low, his singing voice was high, pure as a harp. It sounded almost like a woman's voice. He sang a song in a language

Mattie didn't know. Even without understanding the words, she could tell it was a love song.

"It's Italian," Selena said. "It's about a clown who lost his beloved. Very, very sad."

"A clown love song!" Bell exclaimed, poking Mattie. "That's ridiculous!"

"That's sort of the point," Selena told him. "The clown is ridiculous, but he still loves just like anyone else. It's what makes it so sad."

Everyone clapped like crazy after Master Morogh finished. The ringmaster bowed deeply and walked back toward the wagons.

"He has a beautiful voice," Mattie said to Selena.

"I know. I never heard him sing before." Selena looked uneasy.

Nobody wanted to sing after that, so the music changed to something low and soft. Da and Maya, Mr. and Mrs. Silva, and Sofia and a Bellamy danced a slow waltz. Mattie loved watching her parents together in the fire's glow, Maya's sari whirling out as Da spun her, his arm tight around her waist. The stars gleamed like colored jewels overhead, and the warm breeze pushed the flames this way and that. Selena and Bell sat on either side of her, and Tibby was quiet for once, resting on Mattie's lap.

It was without a doubt one of the best nights of Mattie's life.

CHAPTER 6

For the next three days Master Morogh oversaw the placement of every bench and every rope and guy wire. He watched rehearsals until they met with his approval—three claps of his gloved hands meant he thought the artistes were ready. He made sure the sawdust was strewn evenly and the lights hung perfectly along the midway to show the food trucks and the Marvelwoods' wagon and his own hypnotist's booth to best advantage for the incoming crowd.

Mattie spent as much of that time as she could with Selena. They helped Dee with the dogs, and Mattie taught Tray to play patty-cake with Tibby. Tray sat upright on his hind legs and used his front paws, and he and Tibby both loved it. He learned Mattie's name quickly. She loved petting him and hearing him think, *Nice Mattie, what a good Mattie!* Every time she burst out laughing.

When they wanted to get away from Tibby and Bell, Mattie and Selena would slip away to the Silvas' wagon, which was a lot fancier and bigger than the Marvelwoods'. Selena showed her the bunk beds that folded down at night like the Marvelwoods', only more of them, and a little bathroom at one end that could be hooked up to water lines.

"You can take a shower anytime you want," Mattie said enviously.

"I know, isn't it brilliant? You can come by and use it whenever you like."

Master Morogh's circus had showers in the back yard behind the big top, so Mattie didn't really need it. But there were plenty of times when she'd have given just about anything to have a bathroom in her wagon.

Selena even had a television, though it didn't get any channels. But they could watch movies on it. Mr. Silva was obsessed with westerns, so it was a choice between those and the sappy romantic comedies Sofia liked. They watched a lot of John Wayne, with his funny way of talking. Selena had memorized some of his lines. She liked to make her voice low and gravelly and growl things like, "Don't say it's a fine morning or I'll shoot you." And after Mattie had seen a few John Wayne movies, she could reply with her own quote, in the same voice: "That would cause me great annoyance and displeasure." She wasn't actually crazy about westerns, but it was fun to see them with Selena.

It was fun just to be with Selena. Mattie felt as if she'd known her all her life. They sat cross-legged on Selena's bunk and told each other everything—well, almost everything. Mattie knew about the crush Selena had on a boy in the Florida school she went to in the off season. He was freckled and funny and hadn't paid one single bit of attention to her.

"I'll bet he does this year," Mattie said as she and Selena tried on Sofia's enormous collection of sparkly headbands. Selena was so pretty—how could he not? "At least you've known boys to have crushes on. I've only had them on boys in books."

"It's not quite the same," Selena pointed out, teasing.

"Well, I haven't had much of a chance with the real thing. I've never gone to an actual school."

"I'd hate that," Selena said. "Not that school is so great, but it's fun being with other kids. Even if they think we're a little weird. I do gymnastics at school, and I'm way better than the other girls, but I try not to be stuck up about it, so they sort of like me for that."

"You couldn't be stuck up if you tried," Mattie assured her. She wondered if the kids at Selena's school would like her at all if she ever met them. She wasn't really good at anything, and she didn't have much practice being around people. She'd probably last about an hour in a real school.

She said as much to Selena, and Selena protested, "No, Mattie! You're really funny, and you're nice. That's all you need. And you're pretty, too. I think you'd make lots of friends."

Nobody had ever called Mattie pretty before, except her parents, and they didn't count. She wondered if it was true. The mirror in the Marvelwoods' wagon was old and wavy, and Mattie had never given much attention to what it reflected back at her. She usually just checked to be sure her face wasn't dirty and her hair didn't stick up. She stared at herself in Selena's mirror, her thick hair tamed by a silver headband studded with jewels. Was she really pretty? Funny? Nice?

"Well, maybe we'll go down to Florida with you when you go," Mattie said wistfully. She couldn't imagine Maya agreeing, but she longed for it—even though the idea scared her half to death.

"That would be perfect!" Selena cried. "We have a house there, with a yard and a real television. I have to share a room with Sofia, but she's hardly ever home. She has about a dozen boyfriends. You could come over all the time. I'll work on your parents. I'll get my parents to work on them, too."

Mattie smiled to herself, imagining Maya's response if Mrs. Silva brought it up. The idea of Maya walking around a neighborhood in Florida in her sari and bracelets and henna tattoos, with all the other moms in their shorts and T-shirts and flip-flops staring at her, made her shudder and want to laugh at the same time.

As much as Mattie loved the Silvas' wagon, Selena loved the Marvelwoods' more. The first time Mattie took her there, she gazed in wonder at the thick rugs on the floor, the walls and ceiling draped with printed Indian bedspreads, the curl of smoke from Maya's incense. "It's like a foreign country in here!" she said in a hushed voice, running her hands over the velvety tablecloth. Maya was so pleased by her reaction that she painted Selena's hand with henna right then and there. It was a beautiful design, flowers and butterflies, over and around her fingers and the back of her hand. Selena couldn't stop admiring it. Even Mattie had to admit it looked great— though when Maya offered for the thousandth time to do hers, she said no.

On Wednesday morning the rousties put up a big arched sign at the entrance to the lot that read MASTER MOROGH'S CIRCUS OF WONDERS. Twined through and around the letters were painted animals and human faces, and amazingly they looked just like the circus performers Mattie had gotten to know in the last few days.

"Negyed Bellamy painted it," Selena told her as they stood beneath the sign, staring up. "He's a real artist. He did a lot of the wagons, too. The tigers' wagon is his."

"I love the animals on that wagon," Mattie said, and Selena grinned.

"Good," she said. "Because—well, I can't say. It's a surprise."

"What? Tell me!" Mattie demanded. But Selena mimed zipping her lips closed, and nothing Mattie said would change her mind.

At last it was opening night. The whole circus took part in a March, a parade through town, in the afternoon. It was the first time Mattie had been back in Frog Creek since the breakfast at Audra's. Now townsfolk and farmers lined Main Street, and all the closed-up houses were wide open with people grouped on their front porches, the women fanning themselves in the heat. Mattie had never been in a parade before and it was *fun*. People cheered and hooted as the performers approached, and kids ran up to them and back, their eyes wide with excitement.

The clowns went first, in full makeup, tripping over their huge shoes and doing pratfalls and making the little kids scream with laughter. Behind them was the tigers' wagon, the two big cats on their feet, swaying as the wagon swayed and looking out at the onlookers with their fathomless eyes.

Ahmad walked alongside, his face impassive. Then came Pinga, the old elephant, walking with slow, deliberate steps, and Dee atop her dressed in yellow and blue to match her hair. The dogs dodged between Pinga's legs, barking wildly.

Next came the Silvas in their spangled leotards, the Bellamys making the crowd clap and shout at their tumbling and their exact sameness, and last the Marvelwoods, looking a little ragtag compared to the others. Bell was in his element, waving and grinning at the crowd. Maya moved as if she were in a trance, mysterious and graceful and detached, and Da broke into a jig step every few yards. Tibby was so keyed up that Mattie had to walk with a hand on her shoulder to keep her rooted.

Master Morogh weaved through the crowd, top hat firmly planted, smiling as he patted children on the head and handed parents coupons for cotton candy and balloons. Mattie watched him carefully. Every so often, he would go up to greet someone and take his or her hands in his own for a long moment before moving on. He came to a group that included twin boys, maybe five or six years old, and he grabbed them both by their collars, one in each hand, and lifted them as easily as if they were a couple of kittens. The boys hooted and laughed, kicking their feet above the ground, and the ringmaster lowered them again and bowed.

"Wow!" Bell said, impressed. "Master Morogh's stronger than he looks!"

Mattie nodded in agreement, watching as Master Morogh gripped the hand of the boys' mother. The woman jolted backward and then frowned. Had he said something to upset her? Mattie glanced ahead at Selena, who had paused after a long line of cartwheels. She knew by her friend's puzzled expression that she had seen the same thing Mattie had. They shrugged at each other and Selena slid gracefully into a backbend.

Tibby yanked at Mattie's arm. "Keep up!" she commanded, and Mattie realized the others had moved forward without her.

"That ringmaster is one strange guy," she said to Tibby, and Tibby laughed.

"Strange, strange, strange!" she agreed.

After the March, the artistes hurried back to make sure everything was ready for the opening. Selena's surprise was unveiled: Negyed had painted a sign for the Marvelwoods. He'd had to do it really fast, but Mattie thought it was gorgeous, with pictures of the four Marvelwoods and their names and acts. He'd even put Tibby in the background, which thrilled her just about to death. Selena stopped by to admire it, and she and Mattie watched Master Morogh inspecting his own stage, set up just down the midway. Of course, being Master Morogh, he was dissatisfied.

"My metronome's timing is off!" he fussed, stamping his booted foot in the dust. "I need some help. You, Selena, come here!"

Selena rolled her eyes at Mattie and ran off. "See you under the tent!" she called. "Break a leg!"

"You, too!" Mattie replied, and then had to explain to a horrified Tibby that *break a leg* was what you said instead of *good luck* before a performance and didn't really mean that Selena should break her leg.

The first performance was at seven o'clock. Mattie got caught up in the excitement that swept through the Circus of Wonders when the gates opened at five, and people poured in to the midway for the Come-In, the show before the show. Some of them must have traveled from miles away, she figured. There was no way there were that many people in Frog Creek.

There were rides on poor old Pinga during the Come-In. The little kids sat in the glittery howdah on her back, nearly hysterical with joy. The clowns rode around on unicycles doing things Mattie had never thought could be done on a unicycle. Bub jumped his up and down like it was a pogo stick, and Solomon and Chaz crashed theirs into each other but somehow never fell off. The parrot, Winston, fluttered among them screeching at the top of his bird lungs, "Gentlemen, behave!" The food stands along the midway sold the usual jumbo hot dogs and soda and cotton candy and ice cream, and just past them was Master Morogh's booth, where he hypnotized people. And then there was the Marvelwoods' show.

Da had hung the new sign next to their wagon, between two poles, so it was like a gate. People paid to get in and then stood in a roped-off area in front of a little stage. Da wanted to make a good impression, so Mattie did her trick of wandering through the crowd, touching one and then another, to read what they were thinking. Then she reported back to Da.

"There's a lady who's obsessed with a vase," Mattie whispered to him. "It's big, green, with sort of Chinese flowers painted on the sides. On the front there's a painted Chinese temple. She thinks her son broke it, or else he sold it. She's really mad about it."

Da climbed the steps onto the stage. He moved his hands gracefully, outlining the shape of a vase, and the vase itself appeared a moment later, swaying in the air. Then Da brought his hands down hard. The vase seemed to fall and break into a thousand pieces, which scattered in the air over people's heads and disappeared.

71

"I knew you broke it!" a woman in the crowd cried. "You're such a liar, Daniel!" Mattie had to bite her lip to keep from laughing.

Bell stepped up after Da. He stood very small and still and recited a poem. He had a great memory, so it was easy for him. People looked a little bored as he spoke:

Forward, the Light Brigade!
Was there a man dismay'd?
Not tho' the soldier knew
Someone had blunder'd:
Theirs not to make reply,
Theirs not to—

Right in the middle of the line, he disappeared. Gone. The audience gasped, and then Bell's voice came from the back of the crowd:

—reason why,
Theirs but to do and die:
Into the valley of Death
Rode the six hundred.

The crowd spun around to stare at him, visible again behind them, and Bell gave a sweeping bow to their astonished faces. The applause was deafening. Mattie saw Master Morogh near the back, clapping with the others. Even from that distance, his eyes gleamed. He seemed impressed, his head bobbing up and down in its birdlike way.

After that the crowd was hooked. A lot of them stayed for Maya's fortune-telling and Mattie's mind reading. They took turns. First Maya read someone, then Mattie did. They worked inside the wagon, like always, because they needed privacy.

Mattie and Bell sat cross-legged on the floor behind the velvet curtain and listened as Maya did her first reading. The sweet smell of incense drifted past them from the other side.

"There is a man in your future." Maya's voice was hushed. Mattie couldn't see her mother, but she knew that Maya's smooth, beringed hands were grasping the woman's hands across the table.

"What does he look like?" the woman asked. She sounded both fascinated and wary, as Maya's clients usually did. Wanting to believe, but not really believing.

"He is a little older," Maya said in her lilting Indian accent.

A little older. Bell and Mattie exchanged a grin. That was the truth, Maya's way. "You *know* he's ancient," Bell whispered.

Mattie poked him, putting her finger across her lips.

"But will we get married?" the woman asked, her tone dreamy.

"I see a ring," Maya said diplomatically. "I see many years of happiness."

"Will we have children?" the woman asked. This could get tricky. Mattie had seen the woman come in. She wasn't so young herself.

Maya paused. "I cannot see that clearly. It may not come to pass."

The woman sighed. "Well, you can't have everything, right?" she said. Mattie could hear her chair scrape as she got up. "That was fun. Thank you."

"You are welcome," Maya said. "And . . ."

"What?" Now the woman sounded a little impatient.

"Be careful of the other man."

Bell and Mattie looked at each other again. *Oh no*, Mattie thought.

"What other man?" the woman demanded. "What do you mean, be careful?"

"The one who drinks. Do not get in a car with him."

The woman snorted. "I don't know anyone like that. I have no idea what you're talking about."

Her shoes made no sound on the thick carpet that covered the floor, but she slammed the door hard enough to rock the wagon.

A minute later, Maya pulled back the curtain, and Bell jumped up. "What happens with the guy who drinks?" he asked. "Does he crash his car? Does she die?"

"Stop that!" Maya scolded. "It was nothing. I just had a sense . . ."

"Oh, Maya," Mattie said. "Did you have to warn her? You were doing so well before that!"

Maya pressed her lips together. "Take your next client, Mattie," she said sternly.

Mattie read a heavily made-up woman who was about to get married but didn't want to. When Mattie pointed out the woman's own reluctance, she burst into tears and ran out of the wagon, her mascara streaking down her cheeks. Of course this made everyone who was waiting more eager to come in.

She read an extremely boring guy who was just thinking about work and how hungry he was. Then a girl of about eighteen or nineteen who was jealous of her friend who'd gone off to college. Then a boy who really, really wanted a dog.

"But will I get one?" he kept asking.

"I can't tell you that," Mattie said, very patiently. "I don't see the future."

"Well, what good are you then? You stink!" he shouted, and stormed out.

There was still a line outside the wagon at six thirty, when all at once a tremendous noise started up. It was sort of like music, but not really tuneful. Like an organ, but louder. The people in the line turned toward the big top, and Mattie poked her head behind the curtain, where Maya was waiting for her to finish.

"What *is* that?" Mattie asked.

"It sounds like a calliope," Maya answered, amazed. "I have not heard one of those in years!"

The sound of the calliope drew the line of customers away, to the big top. It was time for the show. The Marvelwoods followed the music, too, watching people stream into the tent. The roustie Juan was taking tickets, and he called to them, "It's a straw house!" That meant sold out. And it was true— there was straw spread on the ground below the bleachers so they could squeeze everyone in.

There was still a little room left, so the Marvelwoods sat in the straw, cross-legged, and watched. The ballyhoo lights crisscrossed the audience in a figure eight. It almost made Mattie light-headed. She saw them pass over a face she recognized: Audra, from the diner at the edge of town. She sat with two little kids, about six or seven years old—the grandchildren she'd mentioned, probably. Mattie waved, and Audra waved back, beaming.

Deafening calliope music played, firing up the crowd. Then the Grand Entry began, the artistes filing into the ring and circling it. The Silvas came first, then Dee and her elephant and dogs. The clowns were behind them, and finally the Bellamys. They spun and bowed, did dance steps and little acrobatic moves, and the audience cheered wildly.

And then there was a sudden silence. Master Morogh came out, dressed in his red coat, top hat, and black gloves. He walked with a peculiar grace that Mattie hadn't noticed before, his toes turned out, his back perfectly straight. A spotlight shone down on him, making the gold braid on his coat glitter. Somehow, the light elongated him. The shadow he cast was tall and almost menacing, and his voice rang out strong as he called, "Ladies and gentlemen, boys and girls, welcome to Master Morogh's Circus of Wonders!" There were cries and hoots and loud clapping, but the audience quieted fast as he went on.

"Tonight you will see marvels beyond your wildest dreams. Beasts of the jungle will terrify you. Daring aerialists will thrill you. The most amazing acrobats alive will astound you. Are you ready?"

The crowd shouted, "Yes!"

"ARE YOU READY?" Master Morogh repeated, his voice echoing in the tent.

"Yes!" they screamed, almost in a frenzy. Mattie was amazed at the way he commanded the crowd. When he fluttered his hands, they swayed. When he raised his arms, they rose to their feet and cheered. It was almost as if he were hypnotizing the whole place, from the blue-painted bleachers to the stalls to the really good seats in the grandstand. Mattie looked around at the faces of the crowd, each one intent on Master Morogh. They couldn't take their eyes off him, though Mattie thought he looked a little silly in his fancy coat and shiny boots.

The clowns ran through the audience, spraying people with water from their giant lapel flowers, falling and tossing each other around, making everyone laugh. Then they cowered in pretend terror as Tray, Blanch, Sweetheart, and Crab raced barking into the ring, leaping on them and knocking them to the ground. Up popped the clowns, each with a tiny dog on his head, as Tray herded them out of the ring.

Pinga came in next, slow and stately, and the dogs came back with her. She did a little handstand on her stumpy front legs, then stood on a stool with her great thick feet, lifting Blanch and Sweetheart in her trunk. She placed the little dogs on her back and plodded around the ring with them, as they stood on their hind legs and pranced atop her. The audience was wild for them.

There was more clown play, one of their set pieces. One clown in whiteface—Bell whispered that it was Bub— wandered around the ring. Chaz, with his big orange wig, approached him, Winston the parrot sitting on his shoulder. Chaz said, "Hey, Bub, wanna make a bet?"

Bub replied, "A bet? On what?"

"I bet you can't do this," Chaz told him. He took out a funnel and tucked it into the belt of his oversized trousers so the wide part was up. Then he tilted his head back and balanced a quarter on his forehead. Finally he tipped his head forward until the coin dropped off his forehead into the funnel and down his pants. Everyone laughed.

"Ooh!" Bub cried. "Awesome!"

"If you can balance this quarter on your forehead and drop it into the funnel like that, you can keep it!"

"I'm sure I can do that," Bub said.

Bub took the funnel and tucked it into the top of his trousers. Then, he carefully balanced the quarter on his forehead. While his head was tilted way back so he couldn't see, Chaz pulled out a jug full of water and poured it down the funnel into Bub's trousers as Winston flapped and shouted. The crowd was in hysterics. Bell and Tibby laughed so hard they were almost crying.

When the clowns finished, the Bellamys came out, leaping and spinning through the air, flipping around the ring so fast they were almost a blur. Once they slowed down enough that people could see they were all identical, the crowd stood and howled. The five of them were moving so fast—twisting and jumping and diving and all exactly alike—that sometimes Mattie wasn't sure if there were two or three or four or infinite Bellamys vaulting and somersaulting. It was dizzying. The audience loved them.

In between each act, Master Morogh came out and fired up the crowd, making them clap and cheer. The food crew strode through the stands, peddling their wares. They were the same group who ran the booths on the midway. They'd paid the circus a fee—a privilege—to sell their food there, and they were allowed to peddle peanuts and ice cream and sodas in the tent, too.

The tigers came after the Bellamys. Everyone hushed as the rousties raised the metal barrier and the cats paced into the ring. Mattie caught her breath. They were so beautiful, the way they walked. Their muscles bunched and unbunched under their striped fur, and she could see their amber eyes surveying the audience with disdain.

Ahmad stood in the center of the ring, all his attention focused on the tigers. He snapped his whip over and over. It made a terrible noise, but he never used it on his cats. At his command they ran, they got up on stools, they rolled, they batted paws in a pretend fight. Mattie remembered the feeling she'd gotten from Hasha, and she knew that the cats hated this.

Maybe they hated Ahmad, too, for making them do it. She didn't even want to watch.

"What's wrong?" Bell asked when Mattie turned away.

"I don't like it," Mattie said. "Those tigers are . . . well, they're kind of magnificent. They shouldn't be doing tricks."

"I think it's awesome," he said. "Imagine working with them! Ahmad must be so tough! I'll bet he's not even a little afraid."

Mattie looked at Ahmad again. "Oh, I'll bet he is, a little. If he's not, he's just dumb."

The audience agreed with Bell, not Mattie. When the tigers padded out of the ring, the crowd cheered even harder than they had for the other acts. They seemed to like the idea of being so close to something so dangerous.

Then the Silvas, the final act, ran out. Up they climbed, fast and graceful, to the top of the tent, and in a minute Mr. Silva and Santos were on their bars, and Mrs. Silva was somersaulting and spinning between them. Stefano took his turn, and Sofia hers, her daredevil twists and spins bringing the audience to their feet. When she hung by her braid, girls in the crowd shrieked, and Mattie knew they were imagining what it must feel like. Then Selena climbed to the platform. She stumbled on one of the ladder rungs, and Mattie thought she must be terribly nervous. She held her breath as her friend stood waiting for the bar.

As she had the other day, Selena swung out and back, out and back, higher and higher. Then, when she reached the highest possible point, she let go of the trapeze and somersaulted through the air. But this time her somersault was wobbly, her body half-curled and awkward in the air. Her father stretched his arms toward her, but she was too far away, and she dropped like a stone.

The audience gasped, and a wave of terror rushed over Mattie, making her knees weak. The fall was so fast, so far! But she'd forgotten the net below. Selena bounced off the mesh as if it were a trampoline and did a quick, shaky flip onto the ground. Relieved, the crowd stood and clapped, and Selena bowed again and again, her teeth flashing white in a grin. Under the bright lights, though, Mattie was sure she could see tears sparkle in her friend's eyes. She swiveled her head and, as the audience took their seats again, saw Master Morogh near the artistes' entrance. His gaze was fierce on Selena as she walked away from the net. But he didn't look angry that she'd fallen, as Mattie would have thought.

Instead, his thin lips curled up in a strange, unsettling smile.

CHAPTER 7

After the crowd filed out, the rousties started to clean up the dropped popcorn boxes and ice cream wrappers. Master Morogh called the artistes together. Away from the spotlight, he was back to his round, irritating self. He rubbed his gloved hands together and said, "Well, well, well! That was a success indeed. A straw house, and I think we satisfied them. Shall we see if we can do it again tomorrow?" Da and Maya nodded and smiled, but Mattie noticed that none of the others did.

"Just a few notes," Master Morogh continued. A general sigh went up. "First, Bellamys—that entrance was a little slow. And you wobbled on the pyramid. And Dee, come on. Can't you make the old cow move just a little faster?"

Mattie was startled. She hadn't seen any of this. And he went on and on, picking apart everyone's work. He even told the clowns they weren't funny enough. It was kind of horrible, watching people deflate after they'd been so pleased with their performances. He didn't mention the Marvelwoods, and Mattie wondered why. Maybe, she thought, it was because they weren't really part of the show. He didn't say a word about the tigers. And he didn't bring up Selena's fall.

Mattie walked Selena back to her wagon afterward. "Is he always like that?" she asked.

"Always," Selena replied. "He'll never just say it was good, even when it obviously was. He's always got to try to make it perfect. It makes my parents so mad! But then Mom says it's a good thing, to strive for perfection. Ugh. I sure missed perfection tonight."

"It's a good thing he didn't hear me tonight," Mattie said. "I made one lady cry and a boy so mad he ran out. He'd probably have sent us packing!"

"You're lucky, being out on the midway," Selena said. "He can't really watch you."

"He was there for Bell's act, though," Mattie noted. "I saw him in the back. I wonder what he thought." Mattie pictured Master Morogh's face, his expression as Bell appeared in the back of the crowd and finished the recitation. What *had* he thought?

She waved good-bye to Selena at her door and said, "You'll get the somersault next time."

"I was sure the timing was right!" Selena fumed. "It was so embarrassing!"

"You'll do it perfectly tomorrow," Mattie said firmly. But she sounded more certain than she felt.

On the way back, she detoured past the tigers. They were both lying down, heads on their paws. She looked at them, trying to figure out what they were thinking. But they both closed their tawny eyes as she gazed, unwilling to let her in.

"Good night," Mattie whispered to them.

Friday morning was leisurely. They ate breakfast in the cookhouse. Without Master Morogh there to criticize, everyone was excited about the night before, reliving the high points and congratulating each other. Rehearsals started right after, and the clowns had the first rehearsal, so Selena and Mattie had time to spend together.

"Let's go to town," Selena suggested. "We can stop at the diner. It'll be air-conditioned, I'll bet. My treat."

Selena's mom said yes, and Mattie asked Da, who said yes, too. She was pretty sure that Maya wouldn't have.

"Be back in an hour," Da warned, and Mattie ran to join Selena.

It was really hot, and they walked to town slowly, trying to stay in the shade on the sun-drenched streets. The air-conditioning at Audra's was lovely, and Audra came out from the kitchen to give Mattie a hug.

"That was some evening we had us last night!" Audra exclaimed. "Those tigers—my goodness! How are you settling in at the circus? And how's that delicious little sister of yours?"

"The circus is great," Mattie said. "But Tibby's a terrible pest!" Audra laughed. Mattie introduced Selena, and Audra got them both ice waters while they slid into a booth and studied the menu.

"We should have ice cream, right?" Selena said. "I want a strawberry sundae."

The choices seemed overwhelming to Mattie, so she ordered the same thing. And when it came, the strawberry sundae was the most fabulous thing Mattie had ever seen. Piles of whipped cream, sprinkled nuts, a round cherry on the top—she almost didn't want to dig her spoon in, it was so beautiful.

They ate in worshipful silence for a few minutes, and then Mattie noticed some kids peering in the front window. There were four of them, three boys and a girl. One of the boys had a buzz cut, and the girl was really skinny and tall. They looked about her own age. The kids pushed through the door, greeting Audra, and took the booth next to Mattie and Selena's.

"Hey," the girl said, turning to look at them over the back of the booth, "are you with the circus?" She had a thick Southern accent.

"We sure are," Selena replied. Mattie cringed a little.

"Cool!" one of the boys exclaimed. "What do you do?"

"I'm an aerialist," Selena said. "I do stuff on the trapeze." She sounded proud.

The boy pointed to Mattie. "What about you?"

Mattie looked down at the ice cream melting in her dish. "Um . . . I read minds."

The boy gave her a funny look. "Interesting," he said. The way he said it bothered her.

The girl laughed. "Can you tell what I'm thinking?"

"Rubes have to pay," Mattie said to her.

"Mattie!" Selena chided. *Rube* was an insult. To circus people it mostly just meant non-circus people, but it also meant a kind of hick. Mattie didn't know why she said it. The kids looked nice enough.

They knew what rube meant, and they didn't like being called that at all. The girl scowled and turned her back. She said something to the others in a voice too low for Mattie to hear, and they all stood abruptly and walked out, leaving Audra holding their menus, open-mouthed with surprise.

"Why did you do that?" Selena demanded. "They were all right."

"I'm sorry," Mattie muttered. "I just . . . they were making fun of me."

Selena frowned. "They were not, Mattie. They were only asking. You need to get over yourself a little."

Mattie would have been hurt if anyone else had said that, but she realized that Selena was right. "I know," she said apologetically. "But I hate it when people ask what I do. They always give me that look."

"What look?"

"Like . . . what a weirdo I am."

"They don't. You're imagining it."

"You know I'm not!" Mattie cried. "People look at us, they say things. We don't fit in anywhere!" She stirred her melted ice cream furiously.

"I do know," Selena said. "I get the look, too, sometimes. But I try not to let it bother me."

"How do you do that?"

"Well, I have my family. I fit in there. And the circus. We've been part of it for almost six years. And then at my school, I've got friends who know what I do. They don't care—or at least they're used to it. Some of them even think it's cool."

Mattie sighed. "I just wish I was normal, from a normal family. Like families in books."

"But those are *books*," Selena pointed out. "Real families aren't normal. My family sure isn't."

"You're a circus family. Circus families have to be weird. But regular families . . ."

"Not them either," Selena said. "Where I live in the winter, there are regular families. Lots of them. And they're all messed up in some way. There's one family who lives near us where the dad's drunk all the time, and about once a week the mom locks him out of the house and he stomps around the neighborhood shouting and singing country-western heartbreak songs. One of my friends at school has a mom and a dad, and three stepfathers and two stepmothers, and not one of them remembers her birthday. There's no such thing as a normal family."

This wasn't an idea Mattie had really considered before.

"So you have to stop comparing," Selena said firmly.

Mattie nodded. "You're right," she said. "I really am sorry. I don't know why I acted like that."

"That's okay," Selena assured her. "Let's go. It's nearly time for my rehearsal, and if I'm late . . ." Mattie was learning that Selena got over stuff fast.

Audra came out with the bill, and Selena paid, waving off Mattie's thanks.

"You take care, sweetie," Audra said to Mattie. "Don't let those kids bother you. They don't mean any harm."

Mattie sighed. "I know. It's just . . . well, it's just hard. I get so embarrassed about my family. My weird mom. Our weird jobs."

"Oh, honey," Audra said, "you've got to be thankful for what you've got. My grandbabies? Their mama left them. Just left them. I'm raising those children. They'd give anything for a mama, weird or not."

Mattie flushed, embarrassed. "I'm sorry," she said, low. "I didn't know."

"Of course you didn't," Audra said. "None of us knows what other people carry. We just have to try for gratitude. To realize when we have enough."

Mattie took this in. Gratitude wasn't something she'd had much practice at. But Selena was right—she had to stop comparing her life with other people's. "I'll try," she said, a little doubtfully.

"That's all any of us can do," Audra said, gathering up the sundae dishes.

At the door, Mattie turned back to Audra. "I'm sorry I made those kids leave."

Audra laughed. "They'll be back," she said. "They can't resist my cupcakes!"

Bell came up to Mattie just after the gates opened for the Come-In. "I want to see Master Morogh do his act," he said. "Will you come with me?" He knew Da and Maya wouldn't let him go alone, and Mattie had to admit she was curious. Scared, but curious.

"I guess," she said. "But we'll just stand in the back, okay?"

Da gave his permission, and they slipped away after Bell's performance and headed to Master Morogh's booth. On the way out, Maya stopped Mattie and said, "Be sure you are back in time for your act. And keep an eye on Bell."

"Stop nagging," Mattie replied, annoyed. As if she needed to be told!

The ringmaster had a stage about the size of the Marvelwoods', but fancier. It was painted gold, with a red velvet curtain strung around it, and was bare except for a little wooden table that held a metronome, clicking and clacking back and forth. There was a woman up there with the ringmaster, staring at the metronome. Her face was blank as her eyes followed the metronome's pendulum. The crowd watched, enthralled. The roustie taking tickets waved Mattie and Bell through. They stood at the back.

"She really looks hypnotized!" Bell whispered.

"Well, hypnotism is real," Mattie said, low. "Some people can actually be hypnotized. Not everyone, though."

"I wonder if I can," Bell said thoughtfully.

They watched the woman do as Master Morogh commanded. She sat on empty air, as if there were a chair beneath her. She did a little dance without music. Then Master Morogh said, "You are five years old. Something sad has happened. Tell us about it." His tone was gentle but forceful.

In a little baby voice, the woman said, "Davy took my doll. He pulled her arms off. He cut off all her hair! Why'd he do that, Mommy? Why?" Tears ran down her face.

People in the crowd laughed uneasily, and Mattie shivered. The woman sounded just like a five-year-old. She must have been forty, but Mattie could see the kid she'd been in her expression.

Master Morogh stopped the metronome and woke the woman with three loud claps of his hands. Her face turned forty again. She wiped the tears from her cheeks, bewildered.

"What happened?" she asked in confusion.

"You lost your doll," Master Morogh told her.

"My doll?"

"Davy took it."

Realization dawned on her, and for a second that old sadness flitted across her face. Then she laughed.

"Wow, I hadn't thought about that in decades! Amazing!" The audience clapped and cheered, and the woman stepped down.

Master Morogh called out, "Do I have another volunteer?" A dozen hands went up. He pointed to a young man wearing a baseball cap. "You, sir. Come on up."

The man mounted the stairs and stood confidently on the

stage, his legs wide, his hands clasped behind his back. Master Morogh started the metronome again.

"Now, observe the pendulum," he said. "Yes, like that. See it go back and forth, back and forth?" The man nodded. "Back and forth, back and forth." Master Morogh's voice changed, lowered. The man's head started to move back and forth with the movement of the pendulum.

"Now you're asleep, aren't you?" Master Morogh asked after a few minutes. The man nodded again. "Tell me."

"I'm asleep," the man said obediently.

"What's your name?"

"Joe Hensky."

"And what do you do, Joe?"

"I'm in college."

"You're in a fraternity, right?" Mattie could see that this wasn't mind reading: the guy wore a T-shirt with Greek letters on it.

"Yes."

"What did you have to do to get into your fraternity?" Master Morogh asked. "Show us."

The man immediately lay down on the stage and crawled across it to Master Morogh. Then he kissed the hypnotist's shoes. The audience started to laugh.

"Is that all?" Master Morogh urged.

The man stood up again. He stripped off his T-shirt and jeans. In his underwear, he ran around the stage, clucking like a chicken. The crowd howled with laughter.

"Stop!" Master Morogh commanded. He smiled at the audience. "We get the idea." He clapped his hands, and the man gave a start. He looked down at himself, clad only in purple boxers, and at his clothes in a pile. Frantically, he tried to cover himself with his hands. The audience went wild.

Beet-red, the man snatched up his clothes and jumped off the stage, running through the crowd as they hooted.

"That was really mean," Mattie whispered to Bell.

"You're crazy! That guy in his underwear—it was so funny!"

Master Morogh scanned the audience again, and his gaze landed on Mattie and Bell, standing in the back. He smiled.

"Young man!" he said, pointing at Bell. "Come on up."

Mattie grabbed Bell's arm, but he shrugged her off and scampered toward the stage.

"Bell, no!" Mattie called after him, feeling a stab of panic. "We don't have time!"

"It won't take long, little lady," Master Morogh assured her. Mattie met his eyes, sharp and knowing below their high arched brows, as Bell climbed the steps to the stage.

"Stand there, and look at the pendulum," Master Morogh ordered Bell. Bell planted himself in front of the metronome, and Master Morogh started it up. *Click-clack, click-clack* it went, back and forth. Mattie watched Bell fearfully. It took only a couple of moments for the light to leave his eyes. Like the frat guy and the woman before him, his expression went slack and lifeless.

"No!" Mattie said again. She started for the stage, her heart pounding. "Bell, come back here!" But Bell couldn't hear her.

"Now, young man, what is your name?" Master Morogh asked. His tone was warm and gentle.

"Bell Marvelwood," Bell answered in a wooden voice.

"How old are you?"

"Nine."

"And what do you do?"

Mattie reached the steps to the stage. She held her breath as Bell answered.

"I disappear," Bell said.

The audience laughed, maybe thinking he meant that he avoided his chores at home. Master Morogh smiled and bent close to Bell. He said something that Mattie couldn't hear.

"Bell, wake up!" Mattie cried. There was something wrong here, something very wrong. But Master Morogh kept his gaze on Bell. He reached out his hand, his right hand, ungloved, and Bell lifted his own hand. Their fingers touched.

Mattie raced across the stage, breathing hard. As she reached Bell, she saw a great shudder shake him from his head to his feet. Something leaped between his fingers and Master Morogh's, like an electric shock, and Master Morogh jumped. Then they were both still.

CHAPTER 8

Mattie stamped her foot on the floor of the stage. "Stop it!" she shouted. "Wake him up!" Bell stood limply in front of her, his arms now at his sides.

"Of course, my dear. I didn't mean to frighten you," Master Morogh said, pulling on his glove. His voice was calm again, and he smiled. He clapped his hands three times, and Bell's face changed.

Mattie looked closely at him. He seemed awake—confused but alert. He seemed like Bell.

"Come on," Mattie hissed, yanking him by his shirtsleeve to the edge of the stage. He stumbled after her, and they pushed back through the crowd, whose curious eyes followed them. Behind them Mattie heard Master Morogh call, "We have time for one more volunteer! Who will it be?"

She pulled Bell back to their wagon. It was time for her to do her act.

"Are you all right?" she asked him.

He nodded. Mattie could see the same bewilderment in his face that had been in the hypnotized woman's and the fraternity guy's.

"You shouldn't have done that," she scolded, relieved. "Go find Da and stay with him. Keep away from Master Morogh!"

Bell nodded again, and Mattie ducked into the wagon, where Maya was waiting, exasperated as usual, with Mattie's first customer. She was an elderly woman with a pink scalp showing through her gray curls and a nice smile. Mattie could tell, just looking at her, that her mind was full of grandchildren, and she sighed. *Boring.*

The next day, Saturday, was going to be the biggest, according to Dee. "Saturday night's when everyone wants to have a good time," she said at breakfast. Mattie knew it was true. It was always the most crowded night for fairs, too. Everyone was excited. Even Ahmad seemed a little twitchy.

At last it was time for the Come-In. The crowds streamed in, stopping to buy their cotton candy and hot dogs, pausing at Master Morogh's stand to watch volunteers get hypnotized, laughing at the clowns as they roamed through, tumbling and fighting and pratfalling. A big audience gathered for Da's act, and Mattie watched from the back as everyone *ooh*ed and *aah*ed when he materialized a castle and the *Mona Lisa* and a Moroccan casbah that some couple had visited on their honeymoon.

Then Bell stood on the stage and began to recite. He'd been pale and quiet all day, and Maya had wondered if he might be coming down with something. He didn't have a fever, though, so he had to go on—Maya's rule. This time he chose his favorite poem, "Jabberwocky." He liked it because it didn't make any sense.

> *"'Twas brillig, and the slithy toves*
> *Did gyre and gimble in the wabe;*
> *All mimsy were the borogoves,*
> *And the mome rath—"*

He stopped at the usual point where he disappeared. But he was still visible. Mattie stared at her brother, bewildered. What was going on?

The audience, unsure of what was supposed to happen, began to murmur, and Bell started over, louder and a little frantic.

> *"All mimsy were the borogoves,*
> *And the mome rath—"*

He stopped again, but he didn't disappear. He stayed right there.

Da took over fast as Bell stumbled down the stairs. "Ladies and gentlemen!" he called, running onto the stage. "I'll take suggestions from the audience. What do you want to see?"

The audience shifted and muttered, but they liked this idea, so they forgave Bell his failure. "A lion!" one little boy called.

"A comet!" shouted a man.

Da moved his arms and a lion appeared, snarling, its teeth long and lifelike. A lady gave a little shriek, and the audience was Da's.

Mattie raced into the wagon. Bell was there with Maya. Tibby stood next to them, her bicolored eyes wide.

"What happened?" Mattie demanded. "Why didn't you disappear?"

Bell's face was white with shock, his freckles standing out almost black. "I couldn't," he managed. "I just couldn't. It wasn't there." His shoulders shook as he started to cry, and his tears set off Tibby, who always cried when anyone else did.

"What wasn't there?"

"My—my disappearing. It wasn't there!"

Maya looked bewildered. "What do you mean?" she asked Bell.

Bell wiped his nose with his hand. "I don't know," he said, snuffling. "You know how you sort of . . . I don't know. You reach inside? And then you can do it?"

Mattie nodded. That was as good an explanation as any for what happened when she read people.

"I reached, and there wasn't anything. It was just gone."

"How can that be?" Maya whispered.

Mattie touched Bell's arm. Immediately she was bombarded by his feelings. The fear, anxiety, and terrible confusion almost made her dizzy. She stared at him.

"I can read you," she said.

His mouth dropped open. "Why? What does that mean?"

"I . . . I'm not sure," she admitted. "You're still my brother. I shouldn't be able to read you!"

"No, that is not how it works," Maya told her. "It is not whether you are related. It is whether you have a talent. If you can read him, it means—it means he no longer has his talent."

She put a hand on Bell's head, and drew in a deep breath as she read his future in the touch. Bell pulled away.

The wagon door crashed open, and Da ran in.

"What on earth . . . ?" he cried. "Bell, what's going on?" Bell started to speak, but Da held up a hand. "Wait, don't tell

me. We dinna have time. There's a line outside for you two—
Maya, Mattie. You have customers. We'll talk afterward. Why
is Tibby crying?" He reached down and scooped up Tibby,
who had curled up on the floor next to Bell and was now
sobbing inconsolably.

"Come on, wee one," he said to her. "You and Bell and
me, we'll go talk to the elephant. Wipe away those tears,
bairn." They were out the door in a minute, leaving Mattie
and Maya speechless.

Maya recovered fast. "You must dress," she said to Mattie.
"Go in the back and change. I will take the first one."

Mattie was full of dread as she shucked off her jeans and tee
and got into her mind-reading outfit. She tried to think what
Bell must be feeling, without his talent. She'd spent so long
wishing she didn't have hers, but actually not to have it . . . she
couldn't imagine.

She listened as Maya read a man who had started a company
that made some sort of fishing equipment.

"You will do well," she said. Her voice didn't betray
anything. It was her usual low, musical tone, perfect for fortune-
telling. "You will make more than enough for the mortgage.
Just be sure your contracts are good. Payment in advance."

"But my first order is from my brother-in-law," the man
protested. "I can't make him pay in advance."

"Payment in advance," Maya insisted. Mattie heard the
man sigh, heard his chair scrape as he got up.

Mattie did her readings in a kind of daze, longing to go
to Bell to hear what had happened. By the time she was done,
she had nearly convinced herself that his condition was just
temporary, and she ran out of the wagon toward the big top
when the calliope started up. Maya wasn't far behind.

They found the others sitting in the straw; the house was full again. The ballyhoo lights swept across the audience, over and over, as people made their way into their seats, and the calliope music was deafening. The crowd's excited faces made Bell's expression seem even more dejected. Mattie's heart sank.

"It's not back?" she asked, sinking down beside him. She almost had to shout to make herself heard over the music.

"I keep trying, but nothing happens," he said glumly. "I feel like I lost an arm or something. It's so weird. I didn't know how . . . how important it was."

He lowered his head to his bent knees, and Mattie took his hand, feeling all his sadness and despair. "Then we'll get it back," she said firmly.

Bell looked up, his eyes alight with hope. "How?"

Mattie didn't have the slightest idea. She just wanted Bell to feel better. Her thoughts raced as she tried to come up with an idea—anything at all. But her mind was blank.

At that moment the spotlight focused on the center of the ring, creating a luminous circle. It wavered and strengthened and then, without warning, Master Morogh appeared in the middle of it. The audience gasped in amazement, and Mattie gasped, too.

All at once, she knew.

The ringmaster, singing at the bonfire with that high, pure voice, just like Julietta. Walking with an elegant dancer's posture, just like Selena. And now this. Master Morogh hadn't been there, and then suddenly he was. Appearing out of nowhere, just like Bell.

Somehow, Master Morogh had stolen their special skills—Julietta's singing, Selena's grace, Bell's disappearing.

He had taken all their talents for himself.

CHAPTER 9

After the performance, Mattie ran out of the big top before the others were on their feet. She waited, twitching with impatience, until she saw the Bellamys coming from behind the tent.

"Maso!" she cried. One of the Bellamys turned his head.

"Hey there, Mattie," he said. "Did you see us? We nailed that pyramid tonight. No wobbles at all!"

"Maso, listen. You said something the other day—something about how nothing in the circus is real. Remember?"

"Sure," Maso said, his forehead creasing in puzzlement.

"What did you mean, exactly? What isn't real?"

"Well, it's a circus. All illusion, right?"

"But is there something specific? Something about—about Master Morogh?"

The Bellamys exchanged looks.

"There've been some things . . . ," Maso said. He lowered his voice. "A few strange things."

"Like what?"

"There were the other tumblers." This was another Bellamy.

"What happened to them?"

"They just couldn't hit their marks anymore. One of them got hurt, bad. She broke her neck."

"Did she die?" Mattie asked, horrified.

"No, but she was in the hospital a long time," the Bellamy replied. "I heard she walked again, but she couldn't tumble, of course. It was pretty awful."

"Were you here when they were?"

"Nope, we came when they left. Can't have two tumbling acts in a circus—that would be war!"

"It was a terrible accident," another Bellamy said.

"*If* it was an accident," Maso said darkly.

"What do you mean?" Mattie asked.

"Oh, there's all sorts of rumors in this place. You know how it is. People say there was jealousy, or backstabbing. That someone made it happen. But that's ridiculous, right?" Maso grinned at her, but his eyes weren't smiling.

Mattie didn't know what to make of this. "Were there any others? Other . . . accidents?"

"There was the old ringmaster," a Bellamy said. "We were there for that one. Morogh was just the hypnotist back then. Nothing special. He did okay at the hypnotism, but not much else. The ringmaster, though—Master Minka—he was a big, big guy. Big voice. Big presence. He could make everyone take notice, I'll tell you. But then, one day . . . he couldn't."

"Couldn't what?" Mattie asked.

"Couldn't do his job. When he opened his mouth, it was just ordinary. No charisma, you know what I mean? We thought he was sick, so Morogh took his place. And Morogh was great at it, just like Minka had been. He had the audience in the palm of his hand."

Mattie closed her eyes for a minute. It all fit. She didn't know how he'd done it, but she knew for sure it was all Morogh's doing.

"Thanks," she said. "See you later, Bellamys."

"Mattie—," Maso started.

"Later," Mattie said. "I have to go!"

"See you later," the Bellamys echoed, and Maso added, "Be careful, Mattie!" The worry in his voice was unnerving.

Mattie ran as fast as she could through the crowds heading back to the parking lot. At the Marvelwoods' wagon, she leaped up the stairs and into the little room, where her family sat around their low table, talking quietly and trying to soothe Bell, who was huddled in misery.

"Da, Maya," she said, trying to catch her breath as they all stared up at her. "I have something to tell you."

"Where have you been, Mattie?" Maya demanded. "The last thing we need is to worry about you, too."

"Listen to me!" Mattie cried. "I know what happened to Bell. It sounds crazy, but it's true. I know it."

Bell looked up, suddenly alert.

"What is it, child?" Da asked, his voice calm.

Mattie took a deep breath. "Master Morogh has been stealing things from people. Their skills. Their talents."

It sounded so strange, so absolutely ridiculous that Mattie knew her parents wouldn't believe her. But as she explained what she'd figured out, described the sword-swallower and

Julietta, Selena and the old ringmaster and the poor broken tumbler, they didn't challenge her at all. Instead, they looked at each other and nodded.

"I had no idea there were ones like him around," Da said at last. "I didn't sense it at all."

"What do you mean, 'ones like him'?" Mattie demanded.

Tibby was following this conversation closely, her bright eyes moving from speaker to speaker. Da glanced at her, and Mattie reached over and pulled out some blocks from beneath the little table where she and Maya did their acts.

"Can you build me a tower, Tibs? Can you put nine blocks up without them falling over?" It wouldn't do to have Tibby asking questions that couldn't be answered, or repeating statements that couldn't be explained.

"I can!" Tibby said proudly, and grabbed the blocks, immediately starting to pile them. At four, the tower fell, and she started again.

Da and Maya exchanged another look, and Da said, "Some of the Travellers are . . . well, they aren't good people. They've always been around. Mostly that type is in Britain, though, not here."

"There are some in India as well," Maya said. "I have heard tales . . ."

Da put a gentle hand on Bell's shoulder. "There's a branch of Travellers that are said to want what others have. They're an envious bunch. Some have no talent of their own, but I've heard tell that they've a way to steal them from ones like us. I've never known any of them, though. I wasn't even sure they truly existed."

"You think Master Morogh's one of those?" Mattie's eyes were wide.

Bell brought his fist down on the table, hard enough to make Mattie jump and Tibby turn briefly from her blocks. "That's what Master Morogh did to me," he said. "He hypnotized me. After that I felt . . . different. But I didn't know why. He stole my talent. He said, 'Give it to me.' And I did. I couldn't help it."

Maya covered her mouth in shock.

"We should go," Da said. "We should get out of here, before he does worse."

"Go?" Mattie said. "And leave Bell like this? We can't do that!" And Selena, she thought. Selena, who'd never be able to do her somersault again, who could get badly hurt, even killed, trying.

"There's nothing we can do now," Da told her. "He knows who we are. We are all in danger."

"Da, no!" Bell cried. Tibby turned again to look at them.

"Hush, hush," Da cautioned.

"No," Maya agreed. "We cannot leave. We must try to help Bell. We will be leaving part of him behind if we go now."

"Maya love," Da began, but she shook her head.

"We must try," she said again. She was determined. Mattie knew that it was nearly impossible to change Maya's mind once she'd made it up.

"Why would Master Morogh want to be able to disappear?" Mattie asked. "What does he need it for?"

Da shook his head. "I dinna know. It can be useful, disappearing. Maybe he did it just because he could. Or maybe it's only his first move."

"You mean he wants . . . more?" Mattie thought of Julietta, and Selena, and all the others. "Which ones does he want?"

"Well, think on it," Da said. "Which ones would give him the most power?"

Making illusions appear. Telling the future. Mind reading. Mattie shivered. "Maya's?" she said, low. "Mine?"

"You'd both do well to stay away from him until we figure this out," Da instructed.

Maya grimaced. "We cannot let him think we're afraid of him. We should just confront him. Tell him what we know. Tell him he has to give it back."

"Nay, love," Da said gently. "What do you know about his kind? You said they were in India as well. What would happen if we confronted one of them?"

For a moment Maya looked frightened, and that just about scared Mattie to death. Nothing frightened Maya. What were they up against?

Tibby let out a squeal—her tower had collapsed again—and Mattie turned to help her. Bell leaned against Maya, his face a mask of misery. Mattie wondered if she was reading his future again as she held him, and what she saw. It was terrible to see Bell like that. He was her little brother, and she was in charge of him. She wanted to pound her own fists on the table, but instead she clenched them tightly in her lap.

They didn't go out to join the others at the bonfire later that evening, and Selena knocked at their door to find out why.

"Bell isn't feeling well," Mattie told her. "Maybe the flu. You shouldn't come in."

"Oh, poor guy," she said. "Can you come out, though?"

"I'm really tired." Mattie wanted to go, to get away from the sense of dread inside the wagon, but she didn't feel like she should.

"Come on. Just for a little while?"

"Can I go?" she asked Da and Maya.

"No, you must stay here," Maya said. "It is not a good idea."

"I wouldn't go to the bonfire," Mattie said. She knew Master Morogh might be there.

"Oh, please!" Selena begged. "We'll just go to my wagon. Just for a little while."

"It'll do no harm, love," Da said to Maya.

Frowning, Maya gave in. "Go ahead then, Mattie. Only to the Silvas' wagon, and only for an hour. And remember what we said."

"Stop nagging me!" Mattie groaned.

She changed her clothes quickly and left the wagon. "Be careful!" Da called behind her, echoing Maso's warning. He didn't have to worry. There was no way she'd get anywhere near Master Morogh.

The girls walked among the wagons, passing by the tigers. Mattie gave them a little wave, and it seemed almost like Hasha lifted her paw in reply.

In Selena's wagon, they pulled down one of the lower bunks and sat cross-legged on it. Selena brought out a bag of makeup and painted Mattie's face, putting glittery eye shadow on her lids and bright fuchsia lipstick on her mouth. Mattie jumped up to look in the bathroom mirror when it was done, hoping she'd look grown-up. But she just looked like her old self, only with way-too-dramatic makeup on.

"I look like one of the clowns. I'm not the makeup type," Mattie said. She rubbed at the lipstick with a tissue. It seemed wrong to be playing around with Selena like this.

"Sure you are," Selena said. "You just need some that's not so sparkly. We don't have any like that, though. It doesn't show up from the ring if it's not really bright."

Mattie sighed. "I have to go back," she said.

"What's wrong, Mattie?" Selena's face was anxious. "You look really upset. Are you in a fight with your mom or something?"

"It's not that," Mattie said, and suddenly she wanted to tell her friend everything. Selena already knew about Mattie's talent. What difference could it possibly make? She sat back down on Selena's bunk. "It's Bell."

Selena's eyes widened. "Is he really sick? Does he have to go to the hospital?"

"No. He's sick, in a way. But it's not like a real sickness."

"What do you mean?"

Mattie twisted her hands in her lap. "Bell's like me, sort of."

"He is? He reads minds, too?"

"No. He . . . disappears. Just like I read minds, and Da makes things materialize, and Maya sees the future." As soon as the words were out, Mattie regretted them. Oh, she was going to be in so much trouble!

Selena's mouth dropped open. "You *all* do stuff? You can really do what it says on your sign? But—but you told me the others couldn't. You lied to me."

"I know," Mattie said miserably. "I'm really sorry. I had to. Can you understand why?"

Selena nodded slowly. "I guess I can. It's your family. You were protecting them, right?"

Mattie felt a rush of relief. She *did* understand.

"Wait, what about Tibby?"

"She levitates. Goes up in the air."

Selena gave a little squeak. "I saw Bell's act. I saw him disappear! You mean he really does it? He just vanishes?" She bounced on the bunk bed mattress in excitement.

"Yes. Well, not anymore."

"What do you mean? What happened?"

Mattie lowered her voice. "We think it was Master Morogh. We think he took Bell's talent."

Selena stared at her. "How?"

"He hypnotized Bell."

Selena covered her mouth with a hand, then took it away.

"Oh no," she whispered.

Mattie had to ask, though she was pretty sure she knew the answer. "Did he ever hypnotize you?"

"It was just for a minute," Selena said. "I'm not even sure what happened."

"When?"

"Thursday morning. Remember? Master Morogh said he wanted to check to see if the metronome was set right. He told me to watch it."

"What did he do?"

"I don't remember," Selena said. "But I felt weird afterward. Kind of sick and dizzy."

"I think he took your gracefulness when you were hypnotized," Mattie said.

"My gracefulness? What do you mean?"

"You missed the somersault on Thursday. It had to have been right after he hypnotized you. You haven't been able to do it since then, have you? And—and he walks like you now."

Selena's eyes filled with tears. "I keep bumping into things," she said in a low voice. "And I twisted my ankle at rehearsal yesterday. Mom and Dad won't even let me on the trapeze. Does this mean I'll never be able to do my act again?"

Mattie put her hand over Selena's, forgetting, and felt a wave of her friend's distress.

"But if he wanted that, why wouldn't he do it to Sofia? She's way better than I am."

"I don't know. Maybe he wanted to be sure she could perform. She's a big draw, with the hoop and all. And it's not just Bell and you. He took Julietta's voice, I'm sure of it."

Selena nodded slowly. "That's why he was singing her song at the bonfire. The one about the clown, remember? She used to sing it all the time. But . . . why is he doing this? What's his plan?"

"I think it's really my talent he wants," Mattie said.

"Oh, Mattie." Selena reached out to put an arm around Mattie's shoulders, but Mattie pulled away. "That would be terrible! But why? What would he do with it?"

Mattie shrugged. "I don't know, exactly. I mean, use your imagination. What couldn't he do, if he read people's minds?"

Selena thought for a minute. "He could find out their secrets. Blackmail them."

"Yes," Mattie said. "He could make them do what he wants. Everyone's got secrets to hide. Everyone."

Mattie could see Selena gauging her own secrets, wondering what the ringmaster would do with them.

"And you wouldn't have your talent anymore," she said.

Mattie stood up. "Well, that might not be so bad," she said. "In fact, that might be kind of great."

Selena shook her head. "Mattie, I know it's hard for you," she said. "But still, your talent—it's part of you. I feel so strange without my grace. I don't really feel like myself at all. And that's not a huge thing like your mind reading. What would you be like if it were gone?" Her lip trembled, and Mattie felt her own tears rising.

"I don't know," Mattie admitted. "I don't know." Would

she be like Bell, sad and hopeless? Or would she be glad to be like everyone else?

She left then, nervously looking around to be sure Master Morogh was nowhere in sight. She could hear the sounds of music and laughter from the back yard. Everyone was still celebrating. And then she heard something that made her clench her fists even as a shiver ran through her: the high, clear tones of a song. She couldn't make out the words, but she recognized the sound. It was Master Morogh again. And Mattie knew now that he was singing with Julietta's voice.

CHAPTER 10

Mattie barely slept at all that night. None of them did. She could hear Bell tossing and turning, muttering and then crying out, and Da and Maya comforting him. Even Tibby was restless, made uneasy by the agitation. When the sky started to lighten outside, Mattie gave up trying.

At breakfast, Maya didn't want to go to the cookhouse, so she made lumpy oatmeal over the burner, and they tried to come up with a plan.

"I must talk to him," Maya insisted. "He cannot hypnotize me. If I can think of a way to stop him . . ."

"He won't stop," Mattie said with certainty. "Why would he?"

Tibby took a mouthful of oatmeal and spat it out, surprised. "Yuck!" she exclaimed. "I want eggs!" They'd had eggs nearly every morning in the cookhouse—scrambled, over easy, fried, always with bacon. Stewie was a genius with eggs.

"Not today, Tibs," Da said, and she got set to howl in protest. A knock at the wagon door interrupted her, and everyone froze.

"Who is it?" Da asked.

"It's me," Selena called.

Mattie got up and opened the door. Selena was outside, hopping from foot to foot with impatience.

"Mattie, I have an idea!" she burst out. "Well, sort of an idea, anyway. It's what you said last night, remember? We have to find out Master Morogh's secret, that's all! You need something to bargain with to get Bell's talent back. And mine. You just—"

"Be quiet!" Mattie hissed, but it was too late.

"Mattie," Maya said behind her. Her voice was dangerously low and quiet. "Mattie, what have you done?"

Selena looked from Mattie to Maya and clapped a hand to her mouth. "Oh. Oh no. I'm sorry. I was so excited, I forgot. Oh, listen, Mrs. Marvelwood, it's not Mattie's fault. I made her tell me. She didn't want to. Really. Oh, crap."

Maya's hand on Mattie's shoulder was like a vise. Mattie didn't need to read her mother's mind. She could feel the anger through her fingers. As Maya pulled her back into the wagon, behind the curtain, Bell's and Da's shocked expressions made her cringe.

"How dare you?" Maya hissed in Mattie's ear. "It is our first rule—our most essential rule! No one must know! Why did you tell?"

"I wanted to!" Mattie exploded. "I'm tired of not being able to say what's real! It's not fair!"

"Not fair?" Maya was incredulous. "We are who we are, Mattie. If the world knew what we truly do, what do you think would happen? Do you want be sent to some government hideaway, studied like a lab rat in a science experiment? Do you want to destroy this family?"

"I don't!" Mattie cried. "Of course I don't! I just . . . I needed . . ."

"You have betrayed us," Maya said. Her face was stony.

"No, I haven't," Mattie insisted. "It's crazy to make us keep our real selves secret! What kind of life is that, when nobody knows who you really are?"

"*We* know," Maya said. "The family knows. Our family is what is important."

Mattie gritted her teeth. "There are other things that are important, too. Friends are important. I wanted to . . . I had to share something. Can't you understand?"

Da pushed through the curtain. "That's enough, the both of you. Do you think we're deaf out here? You're upsetting the wee one, and Selena can hear everything you say. Come on out now." He sounded angry, and that was so rare that it stopped Maya.

They sat on the rugs around the low table, the bowls of oatmeal congealing in front of them. Selena was nearly in tears.

"It's all right, child," Da said to her, his voice gentle again. "What's done is done. We'll have to make the best of it. And it's not the first time we've been found out. Remember, Maya?"

Maya flushed and looked away. Mattie didn't know what he was talking about.

"Your mother told once," Da said. "She had a friend—oh, years ago. Before any of you bairns was born. It was in another circus, in California. A charming woman, Odelle. She was

a fortune-teller, too, but not a real one. A crystal ball type."
Mattie knew what that meant. A total fake. Someone who was
so false she had nearly convinced herself that she was genuine.

"Simon, please," Maya said. Her voice was almost pleading.

"It's important that Mattie know, love," Da said. "And it's
important that you remember." He went on. "Odelle did have
a talent, though, of sorts. She could make people believe her.
And your ma believed she was a real friend. So, eventually,
because they were so close, Odelle found out about us. And
she used the information."

"Used it how?" Bell spoke up. They were the first words
he'd spoken all morning.

"She made a lot of money with it, betting on whether your
mother could 'guess' things about people. And then when
Maya didn't want to do it anymore, when she started to see
the woman more clearly, Odelle threatened to expose us. We
had to run."

Mattie looked at her mother. Maya wouldn't meet her
eyes. She could hardly believe it—Maya had told! She didn't
know what to think.

"Why didn't you know?" she asked Maya. "Couldn't you
read Odelle, to tell what she'd do in the future?"

Maya sighed, clasping and unclasping her hands. "She
changed. When we first became friends and I read her, she had
no plans to deceive me. She was overcome by her greed, and
later by her anger. By then, she was careful. She no longer let
me touch her. And I was foolish—I did not see it." She raised
her eyes to look at Mattie. "When people change, their futures
can change. And Mattie, you will find that their thoughts can
change as well. What is true in someone's mind at one time
might be false at another."

Mattie took this in. She had never really known anyone other than her family long enough to see them change. But it made sense. Her own thoughts and feelings had changed over time. Why shouldn't other people's?

"But I'm not like Odelle. I'm a real friend," Selena said in a shaky voice. "I wouldn't do that."

Maya opened her hand flat on the tabletop. The hennaed flowers and leaves traced a design from her fingertips up her arm. "Will you prove it?"

"How?" Selena whispered.

"Let me read you. Let me see if you will use what you know."

"Yes. Of course you can. Yes." Selena reached out and put her own hennaed hand over Maya's. Maya breathed in deeply.

There was a moment of silence so tense that Mattie was afraid she might scream. Then Maya breathed out. "All right. All right," she said. She turned her hand upward and closed it around Selena's hand, squeezing it. Then she let Selena go.

"She tells the truth," Maya said to Da.

"But now she knows," he said. "You must see that we have to go."

Bell let out a little cry, and Maya put an arm around him. "Your father's right," she said. "It's too dangerous to stay."

"But then I'll never get my talent back," Bell whimpered. Mattie couldn't watch as the tears began to leak from Bell's eyes. He didn't sob or wail or make a sound. He just wept.

"Come on," she said to Selena. "I'll walk you out." Head down, Selena got up and followed Mattie out of the wagon.

"I'm so sorry," Selena said. She was crying, too. "You're going to leave, and it's all my fault."

"Really, it's not," Mattie assured her. "Maya and Da are

sure that Master Morogh will come after the rest of us. He scares them. He scares *me*."

"When will you go?"

"Probably tonight, when nobody will notice." Mattie could hardly keep from crying herself. The circus had felt closer to a home than anyplace she'd ever been. She didn't want to leave. There had to be a way. Then she remembered what Selena had said when she came in. "You had an idea. What was it?"

Selena blinked tears off her lashes and sniffed hard. "It probably doesn't matter now. It was something you said last night. You said that everyone has secrets, remember? I'm sure you're right. If anyone would know that, it would be you." She looked at Mattie, and Mattie nodded.

"So that means that Master Morogh has a secret. Something he's afraid of people knowing—or just afraid of. And if we can find it out, we can use it against him, just the way he would. Like blackmail or something." Selena hiccupped and wiped her eyes.

"But how can we find it out?" Mattie asked.

"We can talk to people about him. Maybe they'll tell us something. And watch him. See what he does."

"We don't have enough time!" Mattie protested. But the idea had taken root.

"We have the rest of the day."

"That's true," Mattie said. "But Da and Maya will never let me wander around. And it's too dangerous for you."

"He's already taken my grace," Selena pointed out. "What else do I have to lose? Besides, I'm very quick, and very quiet. I'll be careful."

Mattie nodded slowly. "It's the only chance we have," she said, though she had her doubts. "I'll see what I can do to get out and help you."

Selena gave her a quick hug and set off on her spying mission, and Mattie turned and took a deep breath, readying herself to go back into the wagon.

Inside, Tibby was howling over her oatmeal again, and Maya looked more frazzled than Mattie had ever seen her. She was so mad she wouldn't meet Mattie's eyes or speak to her. But Da put a comforting hand on Mattie's shoulder.

"We're going to take Bell to the kitchen tent," he said in a low voice. "Tibs has been listening, so we don't dare bring her. She could say just about anything to just about anyone. But the lad needs cheering up, and we'll bring back some food for you and Tibby."

Oh, this was perfect! She could get out to help Selena after all. But Mattie knew she'd better sound upset. "Why can't I go?" she demanded.

Da just shook his head. "You stay here with the little one. We're saying no good-byes, Mattie. We never do. You know that. You can send a note to Selena later on, when we're settled."

"All right," Mattie said sulkily. "Bring something decent to eat. That oatmeal was awful."

"It was, wasn't it?" he agreed, ruffling her hair. Then he, Maya, and Bell were gone.

As soon as Mattie was sure they'd be out of sight, she scooped up Tibby. "We're going for a walk," Mattie told her.

"Put me down!" Tibby commanded.

"Only if you hold my hand."

Tibby snorted, but she took Mattie's hand with her own oatmealy one. "Where are we going?" she asked.

"Want to see the tigers?"

Tibby paused. "Hmmm. They are kind of scary."

"Well, we won't get too close. And Selena will be there."

"Ah, the dear bampot!" Tibby cried in a perfect imitation of Da. Mattie would have laughed if she weren't so upset.

They slipped out of the wagon, looking left and right. Everyone was at rehearsal or busy with their pre-show duties. Clutching Tibby tightly, Mattie weaved among the wagons until she was behind the tigers' cage. Then she peeked around the front to be sure Ahmad wasn't there.

Hasha's amber gaze met hers. Mattie wasn't the least bit afraid now. She could see the sadness there, and in Hadi's eyes, too.

"Hey," Mattie whispered. "How are you doing?" Hasha cocked her head at the sound of her voice.

"Do they talk?" Tibby asked. She pulled back a little.

"Not really," Mattie replied. "But if you look at them really hard, you can sort of tell what they're thinking."

Tibby stared at Hasha. "That one is thinking she would like to play," she announced. "Should we play with them?"

"No," Mattie said firmly. "Never. You keep away from them, okay? See their claws?"

"Sharp," Tibby said.

"Their teeth, too. They're not like kitty cats. They could hurt you."

"Then let's go!" Tibby said nervously, pulling harder at Mattie.

"Oh, look! There's Selena," Mattie said, relieved. Selena was dressed for rehearsal, in her sparkly leotard with her hair slicked back under a headband.

"Mattie! How did you get out?"

"Sneaked," Mattie admitted. "The others went for food."

"Well, Master Morogh's in his wagon," Selena reported. "I climbed up on a box and looked in the window. He was writing something. We can just wait till he's done."

"I have to get back before Da and Maya do," Mattie warned.

"I know. We'll just trail him for a little while."

They sneaked around to the ringmaster's gold-painted wagon and positioned themselves where they could see the door. Mattie told Tibby they were playing spies, and Tibby threw herself into the game, tiptoeing around and staying blessedly quiet as she hid herself behind the big wagon wheel.

It wasn't long at all before the red door of the wagon swung open and Master Morogh stood at the top of the steps. He looked around, and Mattie held her breath and prayed that Tibby wouldn't speak. As usual, the ringmaster wore his gold-striped pants and spotless white shirt, but he was just putting on his black gloves. He held out one hand and started to pull the glove over it, and Mattie covered her mouth to keep a squeak from escaping.

His left hand was missing two fingers.

CHAPTER 11

In a minute the gloves were on. The left and right looked just the same. Master Morogh must have had two of the glove fingers stuffed with something to give the impression of real fingers inside. Silently they watched him walk around the other side of his wagon, and then Mattie turned to Selena.

"What happened to his fingers?" Mattie whispered. "How did he lose them?"

"I don't know," Selena said, her voice low. "I've never seen him without his gloves before. He always wears them. No wonder!"

Tibby crawled out from behind the wagon wheel. "How many fingers does he have?" she asked, whispering in imitation.

"Nine," Mattie replied automatically.

"Perfect!" Tibby announced in a normal voice.

"Shh, we're spies, remember?" Mattie told her. "Let's follow him."

The ringmaster was headed to the big top to watch rehearsals, but he took a roundabout route that confused them. Instead of going directly past the clowns' and then the tigers' wagons, which were closest to his, he walked all the way around the Silvas' wagon and the cookhouse tent. Then he entered the big top through the back door. Selena and Mattie exchanged a questioning glance.

"Let's go back," Mattie said. "I don't want Maya to catch me out here." They hurried to the wagon, Tibby bouncing in Mattie's grip like a helium balloon. Back inside, they settled her at the table with her coloring book.

"So, what did we learn?" Selena asked.

"He's missing two fingers," Mattie said.

"And he likes to walk farther than he has to."

"I'm sure the missing fingers are important," Mattie mused. "Maybe we can figure out what happened."

"Sure, let's just ask him," Selena said, rolling her eyes. "Hey, Master Morogh, did you slice those off by mistake when you were cutting out someone's heart?"

"He did *that*?" Tibby said, looking up from her coloring.

"No, no," Mattie assured her. "We're just joking."

"Ha," Tibby said, and returned to her crayons.

Selena left to go to rehearsal, and Da, Maya, and Bell came back not long after, carrying plates with cold pancakes and sausages. Tibby fell on them ferociously, but Mattie was too nervous to eat.

"We'll have to do the show tonight," Da told Mattie. "We don't want to make Morogh suspicious. But I want to be ready to go right after. We need to pack up."

Mattie let out a sigh. Packing up again. Toys in boxes, drawers sealed so they wouldn't open on the drive, breakables wrapped. How many times had they done it? Fifty, a hundred? She was so tired of packing up. But she made a game of it with Tibby, tossing toys into a box with points for each one that went in and extra points for not touching the sides.

By noon it was so hot in the wagon, Mattie could hardly stand it. "Can we go out?" she begged. "Just for a little while, to get some air? Look, Tibby's all sweaty."

"I *am* all sweaty," Tibby affirmed. "I am very, very, very hot. And also, I am bored with throwing things in a box. I would like to go see the dogs and Pinga and I would like to see the tigers again. But not to play with, like Mattie said." She looked at Mattie, pleased that she had learned the lesson. Mattie froze, afraid that Maya and Da would realize that she had taken Tibby out earlier. But they were preoccupied.

"No dogs right now," Da said. Tibby stamped her foot and rose a little off the floor.

"Tibby, stop," Maya begged. She looked exhausted.

"It's lunchtime," Mattie said. "What if we went to the cookhouse for some food? Master Morogh never goes there at mealtimes. We'd be perfectly safe. We'd stick together. And"—she looked pointedly at Tibby—"she's forgotten about earlier. She won't say anything."

"Grilled cheese, grilled cheese, please please please!" Tibby chanted, bouncing halfway to the ceiling. That was Stewie's lunch specialty, and he made it perfectly, browned just enough. He even added tomato for Bell.

Maya made a sound that was part groan, part shriek. "Yes, all right, go! Stay together. Go on, go!" Before she could change her mind, Mattie grabbed Tibby, and she and Bell ran out of the wagon. Even though it was hot outside, it felt way cooler than inside the wagon, and Mattie took a deep breath of relief.

"Put me down, you eejit," Tibby instructed, and Mattie did.

They made their way cautiously to the cookhouse. There was no sign of Master Morogh. Mattie caught a glimpse of Ahmad walking toward the tiger wagon. She looked away so she didn't meet his eyes.

Selena joined them at the table.

"Have you found out anything new?" Mattie whispered as Selena sat down with her tray.

"No one really wants to talk about Master Morogh," Selena said. "Sal told me that he bought the circus from some guy about ten years ago, and then he hired all new people. A lot of them didn't stay very long. I guess we know why. And he and Ahmad had some kind of fight or something, or else they just hate each other."

"Hmmm," Mattie said. Bell was quiet, picking at his grilled cheese.

"And listen to this. I was talking about Julietta and how her voice disappeared, and Dee said something about a strongman whose strength went."

"Wow." Mattie chewed on her lip. "That sounds like Master Morogh." She remembered how he'd picked up the twins during the circus parade, one in each hand.

"And one more. Some money guy—a stockbroker?—who couldn't make money anymore. Dee said that he claimed it started after he was hypnotized, and he blamed it on Master Morogh. He wanted to sue the circus. But no one believed him, of course."

"You're an amazing spy, Selena," Mattie said admiringly.

The Bellamys sat down at the table. One of them—Oto?—gave Mattie a look as he bit into his sandwich. "You're a secretive sort, you two," he said. Mattie could feel her face turning red.

"What do you mean?" she asked, trying to sound nonchalant.

"Asking all sorts of questions, dodging around. Talking to tigers."

"Are you watching us?"

"Oh, we watch everything," the Bellamy said. "Eyes in the back of our heads, you know." At this, Tibby's own eyes widened. "We keep a lookout for our friends, that's all. Don't want you getting into trouble."

"We're not in trouble. We just like to play spy games," Mattie said, taking a bite of her own sandwich.

"We're good at that, too," one of the other Bellamys said, winking at her. "It's easier when there's five of you."

"Nine," Tibby said, her mouth full of cheese.

"I meant nine," the Bellamy corrected himself. By now, they were familiar with Tibby's numerical preference.

Mattie wasn't quite sure what was going on. It seemed almost like the Bellamys meant something different from what they actually were saying. She remembered that Maso had known a lot about Master Morogh. Maybe they could help, but she couldn't think how. "Well, if we need someone else to play, we'll definitely ask you," she said, a little uncertainly.

The Bellamys all gave her the exact same smile. It was a real smile, times five. "Anytime," they said in unison, and Tibby hooted with laughter, spraying bits of grilled cheese all over the table.

After lunch they trooped back to the wagon. Mattie's

parents were sitting in the shade it cast in two folding chairs, drinking iced tea.

"Want a glassful, girls?" Da asked, holding up the plastic pitcher. "Selena's mother brought it over."

Mattie shook her head. Maya still looked mad, and now Mattie was feeling angry, too. Yes, she'd done something wrong. Again. But Maya had done the very same thing years ago, with her friend Odelle, for the very same reason. It wasn't fair of her to keep on being mad. Mattie was about to say so when a distant shout startled her into silence.

"Get inside, everyone! It's the tigers! The tigers are loose!"

They were all struck still for an instant. Then Maya stood and scooped up Tibby. "Into the wagon!" she commanded. "Hurry!"

Mattie, Bell, Da, and Selena leaped up the steps behind her, slammed the door, and then ran to the windows to peer out. Tibby bounced up and down, trying to push bodies aside so she could see. They heard people yelling from the back yard, and it sounded like they were moving closer.

Then the tigers appeared.

CHAPTER 12

Hasha and Hadi moved slowly but deliberately along the path from the big top to the circus lot entrance. They crouched low to the ground, their muscles rippling like brook water over stones. Out of their wagon, away from the big top, they seemed smaller, but so powerful, so beautiful that they made Mattie catch her breath. Behind them, a considerable distance away, were Sal, Max, Juan, and Ahmad. Ahmad carried his whip. The rousties had their hands full of rope.

Mattie knew the gate at the entrance was closed and locked, but the fence around the circus lot wasn't very high. It wouldn't take any effort at all for the big cats to leap over it. And then what? She imagined the police hunting them through the swamps and forests nearby. She knew they'd shoot the tigers dead when they found them.

Selena was at her shoulder. "Can you do anything?" she asked Mattie in a low voice.

Mattie shook her head.

As the rousties and Ahmad advanced cautiously, Master Morogh appeared behind them. His face, even at that distance, looked as pale as his starched white shirt. In his gloved hand he held something metallic. The sun glinted off it, and Mattie realized it was a gun. She had never seen a gun before, except in John Wayne movies.

The cats were just outside the wagon now. Quickly, before anyone could stop her, Mattie ran to the door, threw it open, and stepped out. Behind her she heard Da shout, and the cats swung their heads in unison to look at her.

She was trembling so hard she could barely stand, but she forced herself to stay as still as stone. It seemed as if the whole world had come to a halt, except for the tigers. Even the breeze stopped rustling the tree leaves at the edge of the circus lot.

She stared hard at Hasha. With her gaze, she tried to send a message. *Remember me?* she asked the tiger with her eyes. *I felt your pain. I feel it now.*

Hasha cocked her head the way she had before, as if she were listening intently. Her amber eyes narrowed, and Mattie held her breath. Then she walked, slowly, slowly, down the wagon steps. The cats were only yards away from her. Nobody else moved.

Mattie held her hand out as she would to a big dog who wanted to sniff her to be sure she was friendly. Hadi stepped back, away from her, but Hasha moved forward. Mattie heard a muffled cry from inside the wagon. Trying to hold her hand steady, she walked another few steps, and Hasha walked up to meet her. The tiger lowered her head a little, and Mattie placed a hand on the warm fur of her skull.

Behind her eyes she saw an image of the tigers' wagon door swinging open and Ahmad standing nearby. Then her mind flooded with sun-dappled clearings and pools, with jungle-like trees and vines and flowers. She saw tiger cubs rolling in tall grass and playing with each other's tails. She felt a wave of hope and longing.

"No," Mattie whispered to Hasha. "It won't be like that. Not if you go now. It will be like this." In her own mind, she tried to create pictures of people scared and screaming and running in panic, of groups of men in the dark with flashlights and guns. She pictured Hadi, shot and bleeding on the ground. She had no idea if the tiger could see what was in her mind, but she made the images as terrible as she could.

Hasha growled deep in her throat, and Mattie was hit with the same awful grief she'd felt when she first touched the tiger's paw. "I'm so, so sorry," she told Hasha. "I'll find a way to get you free, and safe. I promise. I promise. But you have to go back now."

Under her hand, Hasha lowered her head still more, and then she was lying on the ground, and Mattie was sitting beside her. Behind them, Hadi crouched and then lay down as well. Mattie stayed where she was—she couldn't have moved if she'd tried—as the rousties and Ahmad moved forward, step by careful step. When Hasha looked at Ahmad, Mattie could read resignation and a kind of fondness in her. So the tiger didn't despise him after all. Mattie was glad.

But when Master Morogh came closer, Hasha lifted her head and glared at him. Mattie was struck by a wave of hatred so strong that she pulled her hand away from the tiger, shocked. Something in Hasha's gaze must have shown Master Morogh how she felt, because he immediately backed away again, sticking his pistol into the waistband of his pants. He kept going, backing down the midway, until he reached the wagons and ducked out of sight.

Ahmad took over then. He spoke to the tigers in whatever language they shared, and they stood and languidly followed him as he walked slowly back toward their wagon. Before he moved out of Mattie's sight, though, he turned and looked at her. It was a measuring look, like he was trying to figure her out. Then he nodded and turned back.

Sal grabbed her and lifted her as if she were no bigger than Tibby. Mattie's bones wouldn't hold her up anymore. She was as limp as a plucked weed in his arms.

The wagon door flew open, and Da and Maya and the others ran to her side. Da took her from Sal and held her tight. Mattie could feel his heart racing in his chest as she started to cry. Maya stroked her hair, and Bell clutched her hand. Mattie read his admiration and then his fear.

"It's all right, Bell," she said, keeping her voice as level as she could. "I'm fine. I knew I would be. You don't have to worry."

"That was *crazy*," he said, awed. Tibby bounced beside him.

"What did Mattie do to the tigers?" she asked. "Is Mattie crazy?"

"A little bit daftie," Da told her. "But she's fine."

"She can talk to those tigers," Tibby confided. "Everyone is scared of them but Mattie. Even that ringmaster."

"I know," Da said. His voice was full of wonder.

Mattie wriggled in his grip, and he put her down. Her legs were strong enough to hold her up now. "Sorry if I frightened you," she said. "But Master Morogh—he had a gun. I couldn't let him shoot them."

"I can't believe you did that!" Selena cried, throwing her arms around Mattie. At her touch, Mattie read her, too. Like Bell—fright and admiration. "Weren't you afraid they'd eat you?"

"Maybe a little," Mattie told her. "But 'courage is being scared to death . . . and saddling up anyway.'" It was one of her favorite John Wayne quotes, and it made Selena smile.

"Never again," Da said sternly. "You leave the cats to Ahmad. Do you understand?"

Mattie nodded meekly.

"But how did they get out?" Maya wondered. "Someone had to let them out. Who would do that?"

Mattie remembered the image she'd seen when she first touched Hasha. "I think . . . I think it was Ahmad," she said.

"Ahmad? That doesn't make sense," Maya protested. "He's their trainer. Without them, he wouldn't have an act."

"I could be wrong," Mattie said. "I'm not sure." But from what she had seen, Ahmad clearly had something to do with it.

"It is nearly time for the Come-In," Maya said. "Can you do your readings?" Her voice was unusually gentle. Mattie knew that she wasn't angry anymore.

"I think so," Mattie said. Then her mother was Maya again, all business.

"You should get changed then, while your da sets up the stage. He will do his act, and we will do ours next, as usual."

"I have to get ready, too," Selena said. She squeezed Mattie's hand. *Be careful!* she mouthed, and Mattie nodded.

Mattie mounted the stairs into the stuffy wagon. The heat of the day had built inside. It wasn't going to be very pleasant doing readings in there, but at least people would be quick about it. They wouldn't want to linger.

It seemed like there were even more people streaming through the entrance today. It was Sunday, everybody's day off. Mattie watched the crowd in front of Master Morogh's stage. She wondered whose skills, whose special talents he was claiming from the volunteers who raced up, eager to be hypnotized and humiliated in front of everyone.

Da did his act and then took Tibby to the back yard. Bell sat with Mattie behind the curtain in the airless wagon while Maya read futures.

"You should go to the back yard," Mattie whispered. "It's cooler there."

"I don't want to," he whispered back. "I don't feel like seeing anyone."

Mattie pulled out the checkers board, careful not to rattle any of the pieces. Maya's quiet voice was background music to their fierce game, and Mattie was about to jump three of Bell's pieces when he suddenly grabbed her arm.

"Listen," he hissed.

Mattie stopped, still holding her red checker.

"I've been wanting you to read my future," Mattie heard Master Morogh say. She turned wide eyes to Bell.

"Shouldn't you be doing your own show?" Maya asked. She sounded calm. "You don't want to disappoint your audience."

"Oh, I never disappoint," Master Morogh assured her. "My audience is heading for the big top now. I have a few minutes."

"You'll have to take off your glove," Maya said.

"Of course," came Master Morogh's smooth voice.

There was a moment of silence. Then Maya said, "Oh. You want . . ."

"Yes," Master Morogh said. "Yes. Yes. Now you must give

me your power. Will you? Now. Now. Now." His words were steady and slow, like his metronome.

A terrible fear rose in Mattie. Where was Da? She and Bell jumped up, and the checkers flew into the air and rattled to the floor.

Mattie yanked back the curtain but stopped short. Maya sat at the table, Master Morogh across from her. He had one glove off, the glove that had covered his good hand. Maya's hand lay over his limply. In the dim light Mattie could see her face, slack and expressionless as Bell's had been up on the ringmaster's stage.

Mattie shouted, "Stop!" and at that moment something—almost like electricity—leaped between their two hands. Maya rocked backward in her chair, her hair standing out as if she'd stuck her finger in a socket, and she let out a cry that sounded like pain.

Master Morogh looked up and smiled. It was a horrible smile, the same smile he'd given after Selena had fallen, and after he'd hypnotized Bell. His little beard bobbed.

"No," Mattie moaned. Maya blinked, her eyes slowly coming into focus.

"You can't have it!" Bell shouted. "Give it back!" He advanced into the room, trying to look threatening. But he was just nine, and small for his age. The ringmaster smiled again.

"But she gave it to me," he said mildly.

"Get Da," Mattie commanded Bell. "Hurry!"

Bell pushed past the table and out of the wagon. Master Morogh stood up. Maya still sat as if in shock, her hair settling back into place. She looked at her hand wonderingly, turning it this way and that, as if it didn't really belong to her.

"What have you done?" she asked Master Morogh.

"You know what I've done, my dear," he said to her, his tone soothing. "It's mine now. I'll use it well." He moved as if to leave the wagon, but Mattie was in his way. She shrank back against the wall, terrified of touching him.

"Mattie, Mattie, Mattie," he said to her, his words rhythmic, like his metronome. Mattie stared stubbornly at the floor. If she didn't meet his eyes, he couldn't hypnotize her . . . could he?

But that must not have been what he wanted right then, because he walked to the door, which was still swinging open from Bell's rush outside, and in an instant was down the steps and away.

CHAPTER 13

Da came crashing into the wagon, with Bell pulling Tibby just behind. "What happened?" he demanded. But Mattie didn't have to tell him. He saw Maya sitting stunned at the table and flung himself down beside her.

"Maya love," he breathed, taking her hands. "Oh, my dear one, what's he done? Och, how did this happen?"

Maya let out a whimper, a tiny, awful sound. "I was not expecting him," she said. Her voice was thick with tears. "He was so much stronger than I. I never imagined he would be so strong."

Tibby started to wail. Mattie wanted to wail herself. She'd never seen Maya cry before. Maya was the strong one. But Master Morogh had overpowered her so easily!

"It only took a minute," Mattie said in bewilderment. "I didn't even know he was here. I should have stopped him!"

Da looked up at her. "You couldn't have done anything, child. We underestimated him."

"You were right, Simon," Maya said in a low voice. "We should have run when we first had the chance. We should never have waited. We must run now. To save the others."

The others. Mattie knew that Maya meant her. It was she that Master Morogh wanted. And if Maya was no match for the ringmaster, what could Mattie do?

Da put an arm around Maya as she wept and swept the sobbing Tibby into his embrace with his other arm. Mattie caught Bell's eye and looked at the door. He nodded. In the chaos of Maya's grief, they edged to the door and slipped out.

People surged toward the big top as the calliope music rang out. Mattie and Bell were lost among the crowd at once, moving with them to the tent. At the entrance they broke off; there would be no room even on the straw for them tonight. They ran around the big top, sneaking past Master Morogh's wagon and then the tigers'. The cats were lying down, but they were alert, watching with their impenetrable eyes. Mattie and Bell stopped there to talk.

"We have to do something," Mattie said.

Bell shook his head hopelessly. "He's too strong. You saw. What can we do?"

"I don't know," Mattie admitted. "But there must be something. Otherwise we'll leave tonight, and you'll never get your talent back. And neither will Maya."

Bell was silent for a moment. "We can't do that," he said finally. "We can't leave like that."

"We'll bargain with him," Mattie said recklessly. "We'll

force him to give the talents back. I'll promise him mine for yours and Maya's."

Bell stared at her. "But . . . what will you do without yours?"

"You know I don't want it," Mattie said. "I've never wanted it. And it's the only way we can get yours and Maya's back." She tried to sound certain.

"Mattie . . ."

But Bell's voice trailed off. They had no other ideas. It was that or nothing.

The Bellamys came careening around the corner of the tigers' wagon on their way to the big top.

"Come watch from the back," one of them suggested. Suddenly Mattie knew which one it was—Elso. He had a tiny mole on his neck. And next to him was Oto. He had five moles, in exactly the same place. And Maso had two. Each brother had the same number of moles as his name. One part of her thought, *Aha! So that's how Selena knows which one is which!*

Mattie and Bell went with them, entering the big top through the back door. When Selena came back through the ring doors after the Grand Entry, Mattie ran up to her. "The ringmaster got to Maya," Mattie said quietly.

"What do you mean, 'got to her'? What did he do?"

"He hypnotized her. He took her talent."

"Oh, Mattie!" Selena breathed. "Your poor mom! Is she all right?"

"No, she's really not," Mattie admitted. "She was crying. She was—oh, it was awful. She wasn't like herself at all."

Selena winced. "I can't even picture your mother crying. What on earth are you going to do?"

Mattie told her. Selena's eyes grew large with alarm as she talked.

"No. You can't face him alone. You can't."

"I have to," Mattie said. "Do you have a better idea?"

"I just need more time!" Selena grabbed Mattie's arm, not caring that Mattie could read her. Her thoughts were frantic. "I've found out so much about him already. We just haven't figured it all out yet!"

"We don't have more time," Mattie said.

"Then I'll help you," Selena promised. "After the show. We'll get Master Morogh to come to you then."

Mattie, Selena, and Bell watched the performances. Part of Mattie wanted the acts to go on and on so she didn't have to face what came next. Even in the breathless heat that had collected under the big top, she felt frozen when she thought about what would happen when the show was over. She didn't have any clear idea what she would say to Master Morogh or what he would do to her. All she knew was that she had to do something for Bell and Maya, and for Selena.

The last act, as usual, was the tigers. The crowd loved them—the mixture of grace and danger in their act was thrilling. Mattie watched the big cats carefully to see if they behaved differently after their short-lived escape. But they did as Ahmad ordered, balancing on their stools, running in a circle, lashing their tails and growling as the trainer snapped his whip in the air. There was a moment when Ahmad put his turbaned head in Hasha's mouth that terrified everyone, in that way that people love to be scared. *Will she eat him?* they wondered, knowing of course that she wouldn't.

It was all for show, Mattie knew now. All the cats really wanted was freedom.

The applause at the end was deafening, and the entire troupe came out to parade around the ring and take their final bows. The calliope blared, and Master Morogh stood in the center of the ring, the spotlight bright on him. The other spots swept over the artistes as they danced and tumbled. The Bellamys did backflips; the clowns somersaulted into each other, knocking down first one, then another. Selena and her sister cartwheeled in a circle, though Mattie noticed that Selena barely missed crashing into Sofia as they spun. Even her cartwheel timing had gone bad. The audience didn't notice, and the clapping went on and on.

Then, with a suddenness that took Mattie's breath away, all the lights went out and the music stopped. There was utter darkness in the tent, and utter silence. Slowly, slowly, the house lights came up again. The ring was empty; all the artistes had crept out. This was Master Morogh's idea, to make everything more dramatic, more mysterious. Mattie had to admit it was effective.

From behind the tent, Mattie heard Selena call to her, "Master Morogh's on the way to his wagon. We have to go to him—now!"

Mattie looked at Bell, and he grabbed her hand. "Let's go," he said. Mattie read anger and resolve in him, and a fear that echoed her own.

She nodded. It was time.

Bell and Mattie ran out to the back yard. Selena joined them as they tried to figure out where Master Morogh had gone. The wind picked up, pressing them back. It smelled of sulfur and storm-dampness. Mattie couldn't see any of the artistes at first, but then a flash of heat lightning flared across the sky, and in its light she made out Chaz's big orange wig and the sparkles from the Silvas' costumes. A clap of thunder followed a moment later.

"Oh, we'll lose him!" Mattie cried. She didn't want to have to go into the ringmaster's wagon. It was his place, and she was afraid of it.

Selena pointed to the ringmaster's tall top hat, bobbing above the others. "He's over there, near the Bellamys' wagon."

Mattie pushed through the crowd. "Master Morogh!" she called out. She could see him now, his short, round frame halting at the sound of his name. "Master Morogh!" she cried again.

He turned. It was too dark for her to see his expression. They made their way over to him, and then Mattie could see the slow smile spread over his face.

"Well, well, well," he said. "Mattie Marvelwood. What a surprise."

She took a deep breath. "We have to talk."

"Indeed? What about?" Master Morogh looked only at Mattie, ignoring Selena and Bell completely.

"You've taken things that belong to us," Mattie said. "We'd like them back."

"But they were given," Master Morogh replied. "And I want to keep them."

"They don't belong to you," Mattie insisted. "You can't have them."

"Oh, but I can," he said. "Now, get out of my way, children. We have work to do. A storm is coming." He turned away.

"Wait!" she cried.

"Ah, Mattie, Mattie, Mattie," Master Morogh said, turning back again. Mattie met his eyes, green and penetrating under his odd, arched brows. Right away she was drawn in, and she moved closer to him. Bell reached out to pull her back, but Mattie shrugged him off.

"Is it my talent you want?" she asked Master Morogh.

"And what makes you think that I wouldn't just take it, if I wanted it?" he said. He sounded indifferent.

"I don't think it works that way," Mattie said. One of the ringmaster's eyebrows shot up even further. "I think it has to be given." That's what had happened to Bell, and to Maya as well. Master Morogh had asked, and they had given him their talents.

"And I can make you give me yours, if I choose to," he said coolly.

"I'm not as easy to hypnotize as my brother and mother," Mattie said, though she wasn't at all sure this was true. "I'll ask you again. Is it my talent you want?"

"Yessss," he answered, drawing out the *s* like a serpent's hiss. "That's right. You. Your talent. The others' are entertaining— even your mother's is just a curiosity. It's diverting to be able to disappear. It's amusing to know the future. But what can I do with that, really?"

"You could make a lot of money with it," Mattie pointed out.

"I don't want money," he replied.

"You want to know people's thoughts," she said.

"That's right." Master Morogh smiled. "Oh, you're just a child. You have no idea what you can do!"

"But why would you take things like—like Julietta's voice? And Selena's grace?" Mattie asked. Upon hearing the question, something flickered in Master Morogh's face—an expression that reminded her, though she didn't know why, of the sadness in Hasha's eyes.

He gazed at her with a measuring look. "You're a funny girl," he said. "But you would understand, perhaps. You don't like to be different—neither do I. And I was always the one without a talent. The outsider. Now I have them all. I can sing like an angel, I'm as graceful as a ballerina. I have a weightlifter's strength and the power to make my audience believe my every word. I have the ordinary, everyday talents, and the special ones as well. Do you see?"

Mattie didn't see. What did he mean, "the one without a talent"?

"But I don't know what people think," the ringmaster said. "Oh, the power, the utter power of it! To know what others are thinking—who's plotting against you, who's for you—why, it's everything. It's the culmination."

"You might not like it as much as you think you will," Mattie warned.

"I wouldn't worry about that if I were you," Master Morogh said. "I'm sure that I can find a way to live with it. I want your talent. Will you give it to me, Mattie Marvelwood?"

Mattie looked around, at Selena and Bell. On Bell's face she saw a mixture of dread and hope, and she knew what he wanted. She wished Maya were there, so she could know how her mother really felt. Maya would never say it, but would she want Mattie to do what she was going to do?

"No, I won't give it to you," Mattie said. Master Morogh narrowed his eyes, but he didn't speak. "I won't, unless you give back Selena's grace and Bell's and my mother's talents."

"Mattie, no!" Selena cried. She grasped Mattie's hand. Mattie's head was immediately filled with her distress, and she shook her friend off. "He'll know everybody's secrets," Selena said. "He'll know all the secrets in the world."

"I can't help that," Mattie told her. "It's my family. And you're my friend."

"Don't do it for me," Selena begged.

"I will give their talents back, in return for yours," Master Morogh said.

"And you can't try to take them again. You have to leave us alone. All of us."

"Done, done, done," said the ringmaster.

Mattie took a deep breath. "How can I be sure you'll do what you say?" she asked him.

"I swear it to you, on my life," he answered. "You know that if a Traveller swears an oath on his life, he must keep his promise. Otherwise, he'll be cursed." Da had said this before, many times. Mattie hoped it wasn't just a piece of Traveller folklore.

"Then do it," she commanded. Her heart pounded so hard she felt almost sick.

Master Morogh took off his glove, revealing his intact hand. Mattie shook her head. She didn't know where she got the nerve, or even why she did it, but she said, "The other hand."

For a moment there was total silence. The four of them were alone in the space between the wagons. Master Morogh gritted his teeth. Then he pulled off the other glove and held out his three-fingered hand. Despite herself, Mattie gasped.

"Look at me, child," Master Morogh said. "Look into my eyes. Look hard. Look long. Look. Look. Look."

Mattie looked. His eyes changed from green to gray and back again. They darkened, and she felt herself sinking into their depths. From far away, she heard another thunderclap, one loud enough to shake the wagons. She was filled with dread, and she wondered, *Is this how Bell felt? Is this what happened to Maya? Oh, what will be left of me when he's done?*

As if she were sleepwalking, Mattie extended her hand, and the ringmaster reached out to her. And their fingers touched.

CHAPTER 14

Mattie felt an agonizing shock, as if she'd touched a live wire. A whole slew of images raced through her mind, almost like a movie on fast-forward, but she couldn't focus on them. All she could think of was how much it hurt. Oh, it hurt! It was like her insides were being sucked out through her fingers, where they touched Master Morogh's. She couldn't breathe at all. It seemed to last forever. The dark sky flickered overhead, and then Master Morogh pulled his hand away, and she fell backward into Bell's and Selena's arms. She could see their faces above her. They wavered wildly, like images in a funhouse mirror. And then she saw nothing, nothing at all.

When she opened her eyes, she was lying on the floor in her own wagon with her head in Maya's lap. The ringmaster was gone. The room spun around her.

"Did it work?" Mattie whispered.

Bell danced into her line of sight. "Look, Mattie!" he crowed. He disappeared, then reappeared again.

Mattie closed her eyes against the dizziness.

"Maya?" Mattie said.

"What did you do, child? Oh, what have you done?" Maya leaned over, her long hair tickling Mattie's face.

"I did it for you," Mattie said. "For you and Bell. I had to."

Da's face swam into view. "Mattie, Mattie. There's more at stake than just the family."

"I know, Da," Mattie said. "But it's the family that matters most." She was almost surprised to hear herself say it—and to know, with absolute certainty, that it was true.

"Are you all right?"

Mattie wanted to say yes, but she wasn't. She was all wrong. "Where is everyone?"

"They're securing the tents. There's a storm coming."

Now she could hear it—the wind outside the wagon, strong enough to rock it a little on its wheels, and the thunder she'd heard before, closer. A flash of lightning outside the window stabbed into her skull, and she moaned.

"Mattie, are you sick?" Tibby said. Mattie turned her head gingerly and saw her sister sitting cross-legged next to her.

"Maybe a little, Tibs," she said weakly.

"Oh no," Tibby crooned, placing a sticky hand on Mattie's forehead. "That bad man did it. That bad, bad, bad man."

"Don't say things nine times anymore," Mattie said to her. "That's what he does." Tibby nodded, her face serious.

"You're a brave lass," Da said. He sounded exhausted.

"I was afraid, Da."

"That makes your courage all the greater," he told her.

"And Bell says that Morogh swore on his life that he wouldn't harm us again."

"Yes," Mattie said dully. She could see, now that the vertigo was easing, that the light had come back into Maya's eyes, and into Bell's. They looked like themselves again. She tried to be glad for them. Then she tried to figure out why she wasn't glad. After all, she'd always said she didn't want to read minds. And now she couldn't. But thinking felt like swimming through river mud, and she ached with tiredness.

"Do we have to leave tonight?" she asked Da. "I'm not feeling very good."

"We can wait," he said. "Tomorrow is soon enough. The ringmaster won't be bothering us now that he has what he was after. Oh, Mattie . . ."

"It was the only way," Mattie said. "It was my talent he wanted most. He wouldn't have stopped till he got it."

"I never asked you to," Maya murmured. "I would never have."

Mattie put a hand up to her mother's cheek. "I know you didn't. I know that. Don't blame yourself, Mama." Mattie hadn't called Maya that since she was Tibby's age, and it made her mother's tears spill over. Mattie could hardly bear it.

"Can I go to sleep?" she asked Maya. Maya raised her up and helped her undress and put on her pajamas and climb into her bunk.

"Rest now, jaani," she said. *Jaani* meant sweetheart in Hindi. Maya never used words like that.

Mattie turned her back, and in an instant she was asleep. But her mind didn't seem to rest at all. It dreamed and dreamed, and the dreams were of being lost in a new town, and losing Tibby in a grocery store, and misplacing her socks at a laundromat. The one that woke her up was losing all her hair in one great clump that lay on the floor and seemed to breathe, in and out, in and out.

She lay very still, trying to quiet her wild heart. She didn't need dreams to tell her that she'd lost something. She tried to figure out where exactly the emptiness was, but she couldn't pinpoint it. She only knew that there was a hole, a big hole, a black hole, like Maya had taught her about in their science studies, and it moved around inside her until it seemed like every important part of her had been drawn into it.

There was a hard rap at the door of the wagon, and Mattie started. Wasn't it the middle of the night? But Da and Maya were both awake, sitting together and talking in low voices. Da went to the door, Maya behind him. Mattie climbed out of her bunk and peered through the curtain. The five Bellamy brothers stood outside, all equally sodden with the rain that Mattie could hear pelting against the tin roof.

"Bellamys!" Da said. "What can we do for you?" He stepped back to let them in. There was barely enough room in the wagon for the brothers, thick and hulking as they were. Maya pushed through the curtain to find towels, and Mattie handed her two threadbare ones.

"Sorry it's so late," said a Bellamy—Mattie could see it was Oto. "We had to tend to the tents before the storm. But we wanted to know how Mattie was. We saw you carrying her. Did she fall? Is she sick?" He took the towel Maya offered and dried his wet head and face, then handed it to one of his brothers.

"Mattie's fine," Maya said. But the tremble in her voice made her statement unconvincing.

Mattie came into the main room. "I'm all right," she said.

The Bellamys all flashed her the same smile, but it didn't reach their eyes.

"We know there's something going on with Morogh," Elso said, taking his turn with the towel. "That man's not to be trusted. Do you have history with him?"

"Nay," Da said. "Not history. Not exactly."

"Simon," Maya said in warning.

"They should know, love. Who's to say that Morogh won't turn on them, hurt them the way he did those other tumblers? And what's the harm now? We're leaving. We'll not see these folk again."

"You're going?" Negyed said. "Before the final night? Leaving us all in the lurch?"

"You do not need us," Maya said. "We will not be missed."

"That's where you're wrong," Maso said.

"You do not understand. We must go! The children are not safe here anymore," she insisted.

The brothers looked at her, alert and interested, and Da sighed wearily. "Sit, Bellamys. We haven't chairs enough, but sit. And we'll tell you a story."

The Bellamys sank cross-legged to the carpet, and Mattie joined them. Bell and Tibby woke up at the sound of voices and came out, jostling for a place close to Maya. And then Da told the brothers everything.

The looks that crossed their faces would have been funny under other circumstances. In quintuple, they were astonished, fearful, bewildered. They stared at each Marvelwood in turn as Da described their talents, and then they stared at each other, amazed. Mattie was almost as amazed that Da was telling them. She and Bell exchanged glances with each gasp or muffled exclamation from the Bellamys. Maya sat as still as a statue, Tibby on her lap.

"Well," Oto said when Da was finished. "That's quite a story. We knew the man wasn't to be trusted, that there was something. We'd seen things over time, strange things. But we couldn't quite put it all together. And we'd never have guessed about you and your—your—"

"I levitate," Tibby said proudly, and she rose, still cross-legged, a few inches off Maya's lap.

"So you do." Oto shook his head in wonder. "Boy, if I could do that . . ."

"You'd just float around, even lazier than you are now," Harma finished, and his brother jabbed him in the shoulder, hard, while Tibby giggled.

"So what can we do?" Elso asked. "How can we help you?"

"There's nothing to be done," Da said. "Our Mattie did what was needed when she traded her talent away."

Mattie knew she should have felt pride at his words, but she didn't. She just felt tired, and empty.

"And will he keep his promise?" Maso asked. "And not take others' skills?"

"He must," Da said. "It's a Traveller curse if he dinna."

"But we have to get Mattie's talent back," Harma insisted. "He's got far too much power with that. If he can read minds, who knows what he'll do?"

"We'll force him to give it back," Negyed said.

"We'll kidnap him," Oto added.

"We'll threaten him," Maso said.

"We'll feed him to Dee's elephant," Harma said.

"Elephants eat *people*?" Tibby asked, and even Mattie had to laugh a little.

It was very late by the time the Bellamys stood to leave. Tibby was long asleep in Maya's arms. The brothers wanted to confront Master Morogh directly, though Maya protested. Negyed insisted that the ringmaster would back down if the whole circus threatened him, but Mattie had her doubts.

"We'll have to involve the others," Oto pointed out, and Da nodded reluctantly. "They're very fond of you lot, you know. You shouldn't worry."

"Not worry?" Maya said. "When what they know about us could be worth money—or more?"

The brothers stood at the open wagon door as the rain poured down outside. "You have a pretty low opinion of us, don't you?" Harma said to Maya, and she flushed. "We take care of our own here. I'm sorry if we haven't made that clear to you—or if you haven't felt like you were one of our own. But you are, whether you like it or not."

Maya bit her lip. "No, I am the one who is sorry. You have been nothing but welcoming and kind to us. I only . . . well, we have always kept to ourselves. Our secret has always been ours alone. It is very hard for me to know it is out in the world."

"It's not out in the world, not at all," Harma assured her. "It's amongst friends, that's all. We'll keep your secret, I swear to you."

Maya smiled at him then, her real smile, and its brightness made the five Bellamys blink in surprise and then smile back in pleasure before they plunged back out into the raging storm.

CHAPTER 15

"**L**et's sleep," Da said, closing the door. "It's very late, and we've quite a day coming."

Maya tucked Mattie into bed, smoothing her hair from her face. "You'll feel better in the morning," she said.

"*You* didn't, when you lost your talent," Mattie pointed out.

"No," Maya said. "But you did not want yours. We are different in that way, it seems."

"No, we're not," Mattie admitted in a low voice. "I was wrong. I didn't know."

Maya touched Mattie gently on the cheek. "Try to rest," she said.

It wasn't long until the wagon was full of the sounds of sleep. But Mattie had slept so deeply before the Bellamys came that now she was wide awake. She could hear the funny whuffling noise Da made instead of a snore. Maya always slumbered in silence, so Mattie could only hope she was asleep. Carefully she climbed out of her bunk, changed into jeans and a T-shirt and sneakers, tiptoed to the door, and pulled it open.

She was shocked by the gust of wind that yanked the door out of her hand and slammed it against the wagon wall. It made so much noise that she was sure everyone would wake up. But there was no sound behind her, so she stepped out, grabbed the knob, and forced the door closed.

Mattie had no idea what time it was, but there were lights on in a few of the wagons, including the Silvas'. She pushed against the wind and pelting rain, which soaked through her clothes in just a few moments, and arrived at the spot at the Silvas' wagon that she thought might be outside Selena's bunk. Then she rapped, very gently, on the wall.

When no one answered she rapped again louder, and then louder still. A head poked out of the window above her— Sofia. Even with her face puffy with sleep, she was gorgeous.

"Hey, Mattie, what are you doing up?" she whispered.

"Can you get Selena?" Mattie said. The rain in her eyes made her blink hard when she looked up.

Sofia disappeared back inside, and a moment later the wagon door opened and Selena came out. Mattie didn't know how Selena knew not to say anything, but she did. She just wrapped her arms around Mattie and hung on.

Mattie didn't cry. Her face was so wet that Selena probably thought she was crying, but her feelings were too complicated for tears. It was so weird to touch someone and not be able to read her thoughts. It just felt completely and entirely wrong.

Finally Selena let her go. She was completely soaked now,

too. When she spoke, she said exactly the right thing. "You still know what I'm thinking," she said. "You know you do."

Mattie stared hard at her. After a minute, she realized Selena's words were true. Her face showed everything. She was sorry, she was sad. But it was clear that she was glad Mattie was okay.

"Do you want to come inside?" Selena said. "We can be really quiet. No one will mind."

"Is it okay if we don't?" Mattie asked.

"Huh. Well, we might get wet if we stay out here."

Mattie looked at Selena's dripping hair and down at her own sodden clothes, and suddenly she was laughing. It was a little hysterical, but still, she laughed. It felt good.

A bright flash and a tremendous crack of thunder made both girls jump. "We should probably go somewhere, though," Selena added. "Or we might get fried by lightning."

She took Mattie's hand, and they ran around the wagons until they came to the tigers'. There was a canvas drape over the bars to keep the cats from getting wet, so Mattie couldn't see them. The girls crawled under the wagon and leaned back on their elbows. It was a little muddy, but drier. Mattie liked knowing Hasha and Hadi lay right above them.

"Is it back?" Mattie asked. "Your grace—can you feel it?"

"Yes," Selena said. "I did a backflip earlier—the first time I haven't fallen since Thursday. Since he hypnotized me."

"I'm glad," Mattie said.

"Do you want to talk about it?" Selena asked. Mattie nodded, and Selena said, "What happened, exactly?"

"Master Morogh touched me." Mattie stopped for a second. "And it was like—well, like getting hit by lightning, I guess. And it hurt. I fainted, or passed out, or something."

"I know," Selena said. "It was really scary. I thought you were dead for a minute. Bell ran to get your parents, and they came a few minutes later. Tibby went a little nuts."

"She did? What did she do?"

"She was screaming and crying. We were all so scared. Your parents were trying to wake you up, and Bell and I were trying to quiet Tibby down, and the Bellamys were there. Master Morogh was just gone."

Mattie was quiet, imagining the scene.

"How . . . how do you feel?" Selena asked.

Mattie thought about it. "I don't know, exactly. I feel wrong, like something is missing. I feel . . . kind of awful."

"I get it, a little at least," Selena said. "I felt that way. I couldn't even do a cartwheel right. I almost fell off the ladder yesterday. Only it's worse for you, probably."

"It's like Bell said: I didn't know how important it was."

"Well, it was a part of you," Selena said.

"That's what Maya always told me," Mattie said miserably. "I hate that she was right."

"She's your mom," Selena pointed out. "She has to be right sometimes."

They sat quietly for a minute. The wind gusted under the wagon, and Mattie shivered in her wet clothes.

"I want it back!" she cried suddenly. "I want it back!"

Selena nodded, as if she'd expected Mattie to say that. "Then we should figure out how to get it back."

"The Bellamys are trying to figure out how," Mattie said wearily. "But they don't have any real ideas—except for telling the others about Master Morogh."

"Wait, the Bellamys know?"

"They know everything. Da told them."

"Wow," Selena said. "And if they tell the others, everyone will know. Your mom can't be too happy about that."

Mattie had to laugh. "Not too happy, no."

Their voices—or maybe the storm—had disturbed the cats. Mattie could hear them moving in the wagon above. Their big paws padded softly back and forth, back and forth. The sound made her almost remember something, and she thought really hard.

"I saw things," she said, almost to herself.

"What do you mean?"

"When I touched Master Morogh. I saw things. I read him, for just a few seconds before he took it away."

The lightning flashed above, revealing Selena's wide eyes. "What did you see?" Her voice was hushed.

"I'm trying to remember. There was so much, and it went so fast! It was almost like his whole life, like a movie on fast-forward. There was a baby, crying and crying. Do you think it was his baby?"

"I'm sure he doesn't have a baby," Selena said. "Maybe it was him when he was little."

"And then later a boy who was really dirty. Playing in the dirt, by himself. He had a bloody nose. And there was a feeling—he was different."

"Different?"

"I think he was the only who didn't have a talent. Usually it runs in families, like mine, but he wasn't like the others. People were making fun of him."

Selena was quiet.

"He told me he was different, remember? I think his difference was being normal," Mattie said. "Maybe his people really were innkeepers, like he said, but still Travellers with talents. And he had nothing. Maybe the other Traveller kids teased him and beat him up—until he found out he could steal talents."

"What else did you see?"

"There were some weird places. Some traveling fairs, in Scotland maybe. A boat. A jungle-y place. And . . . oh, God."

"What? Tell me!"

"The tigers. In the jungle. Hasha . . ." Mattie stopped. Oh, it was horrible.

"What? What happened?" In her excitement, Selena forgot where they were and tried to sit up, whacking her head on the underside of the wagon. "Ouch!"

"It was Hasha. She did it. She bit off his fingers." Mattie closed her eyes, but the image was still there.

"Oh, gross!" Selena cried. "Why did she do it?"

"I couldn't see that part . . . or maybe I don't remember it. I don't know," Mattie said.

"I know why she did it." The voice came from outside their little space under the wagon. They froze.

Ahmad bent to peer at them. His turban sagged, wilting from the rain. "Come out and get dry," he said. "Come on, both of you. It is not safe to be out in this storm."

Selena and Mattie looked at each other. Somehow, after the tigers' escape, Ahmad didn't seem as scary to Mattie as he had before. They crawled out and meekly followed him to his wagon next door.

Inside, it was warm and dry. There was a thin gold-colored rug on the floor, and just a few pieces of wooden furniture. The girls stood and dripped while Ahmad rummaged through a wooden trunk carved with vines and flowers, then pulled out two T-shirts and two pairs of sweatpants. Mattie was kind of surprised that he would have such ordinary-looking clothes.

"Here, change," he said, and ducked back out into the rain so they'd have privacy.

Quickly they shucked off their sopping clothes and pulled on the shirts and pants he'd given them, rolling up the sleeves and legs. They left their soaked things in a little pile by the door.

Mattie opened the door. "Okay," she said to Ahmad. He came back in. He wasn't too wet; maybe the rain was letting up a little.

"Sit," he said, motioning to two wooden chairs. They were shaped like wide *v*'s, with beautifully carved slats. Nice to look at, not so comfortable. But they sat, leaning back, and Ahmad sat on a third, straight-backed chair. He unwrapped his dripping turban and draped it carefully over the back of the chair. Mattie saw that he wore his hair in a sort of bun on top of his head.

"The Bellamys came by and told me all," Ahmad said to Mattie. "And I witnessed what you did for your family. It was most courageous." His tone was formal, but his voice was warm.

"You were there?" Mattie asked. "I don't remember you being there."

He leaned forward, clasping his hands. "I was watching. I almost stopped you. But I could do nothing to help, not anymore."

Mattie stared at him. "What do you mean, not anymore?" she said.

"What do you mean?" Selena echoed. "Are you—are you one of them? Like Mattie and her family?"

"Once I was," Ahmad said. "Long ago, or so it seems. But Morogh took that from me."

"What was your talent?" Mattie asked, almost in a whisper.

His eyes were sorrowful. "It was like yours, but only with animals. I communicated with animals. Not in words, exactly, but—well, you know. In Sumatra, many of us could do it. It was almost . . . ordinary. I was just a farmer, chickens mostly, and it was useful on the farm."

"What happened?" Selena asked.

"Morogh came there. I don't know how. He wanted tigers, and he asked the people in my village to help him. Our tigers are small and very rare, you see, and not so dangerous as the big Bengals. But dangerous enough. We refused, of course, so he went into the forest himself. I happened upon him there a few days later. I was with my young son."

He paused for a moment, remembering. His expression, usually so impassive, was pained. "Morogh was struggling with Hasha. He had a pistol, but the cat had already taken his fingers when I stepped into the clearing where they fought. He grabbed my son with his bloody hand and said he would kill the boy if I didn't trap Hasha and Hadi."

Yes, this was what Mattie had seen. The scene in the forest, Master Morogh struggling with the tiger. The horror of it.

Ahmad's face twisted. "What could I do? I had to save my son!"

"Of course you did! You didn't have a choice!" Selena assured him.

"I used my power to capture the tigers. I convinced them that they would be safe if they went into the crates Morogh had brought to the forest's edge. None of us, the villagers, had ever lied to them before. We lived in peace with the cats—they had their place, and we had ours. So they went willingly. Then, when they realized what I had done and I . . . I explained to them why I had to do it, they did not blame me. They understood, especially Hasha. Tigers love their cubs as well. They trusted me. They trust me still." He said this bitterly.

"And then, once the tigers were trapped, Morogh hypnotized me. I did not have the strength to resist him. He forced me to give my power up, and he said he would do the same to the other villagers unless I went with him, him and the tigers. We came here, to the circus."

"So Master Morogh has your talent? He can speak with the animals?" Mattie frowned in confusion. She knew that the tigers despised Master Morogh. Even the dogs avoided him.

"Animals are smart, in their way, and they have their own power. He could not bend them to his will. He knows what they think, and they know his mind. But he cannot force them to act. That is why he needs me, to control the tigers. I had to go with him. I have not seen my family since we left. My boy—he is nearly twelve now. My wife . . ." His voice broke.

"I'm so sorry," Mattie said. Sorry for what had happened to him, sorry for not trusting him. Then she thought of something. "Wait, was it you who let the tigers out?"

He sighed. "Yes, it was I. I suppose it was not a sensible thing to do. But we were near the end of our stay here, and I had had enough. This place is very like our forest in Sumatra, so I hoped they might survive here. I thought that if the cats were gone, Morogh would let me leave as well. But I did not think far enough ahead."

"They would have been hunted down," Mattie said. "People wouldn't have understood."

"Yes. I realized that when I saw Morogh with his gun." Ahmad was quiet for a moment. Then he looked up at Mattie. "Even though I did not often use my power—my talent, you call it—I still miss it. It was part of me. So I know how you feel. But more than that, I miss my home and my people. Once

I thought I could get my power back from Morogh, but now I would be satisfied to go without it. I only want to go home."

Mattie drew in a deep breath. "But . . . but we can get it back," she said. Her head was spinning, and it wasn't the dizziness she'd felt earlier. "And we can stop him from doing what he wants to do."

Master Morogh, going out of his way to avoid the tigers' wagon.

Tibby, saying, "Everyone is scared of them but Mattie. Even that ringmaster."

Hasha, her teeth closing on flesh and bone.

Selena tried to struggle out of the deep wooden chair. "What? How can we do that?"

"We have power over Master Morogh," Mattie said. "We know what he's afraid of."

They both looked at her. Slowly, Ahmad nodded his head. "Yes, you are quite right," he said. "We do."

"We do?" Selena's face was filled with curiosity, so Mattie told her.

"He's afraid of the tigers," she said. "He's deathly afraid of the tigers."

CHAPTER 16

They needed a plan. And Mattie needed food. Her stomach was so empty it hurt; she hadn't eaten in as long as she could remember. Ahmad brought them peanut-flavored chips and some very weird cheese and fizzy water. They ate and drank in silence for a few minutes. After that Mattie felt much better.

"These are good," she said, crunching the last chip in the bag. They tasted a little stale, but she was starving.

"I found them in a little grocery," Ahmad told her. "They are from Sumatra—a familiar taste for me. Like home."

Selena took a big swallow of water and hiccupped. "I don't even know where Sumatra is."

Mattie pictured the world map that Da always conjured

up when they were studying history or geography. "Asia someplace, right?"

"It is an island, part of Indonesia," Ahmad said. "It is very far from here and very, very beautiful." His voice was full of sorrow.

Selena changed the subject. "So we have to get the tigers to go after Master Morogh," she said. She had a gleam in her eye that made Mattie nervous.

"I do not think we will have trouble convincing them," Ahmad assured her.

"But you can't communicate with them anymore," Mattie pointed out. "And neither can I now."

"We still communicate, in our way," Ahmad said. "That is why I can control them in the ring. When I speak to them, they understand a little, the way Pinga and the dogs understand Dee. It is not the same as it was before, but it is something. I believe I can get them to understand what we want to do."

"Good," Mattie said. "Then all we have to do is get them in the same place as Master Morogh."

Ahmad held up a finger. "Hush," he said in a low voice. "What is that?"

They all listened hard. There was a strange sort of scratching at the door.

"A tree branch?" Selena whispered. She and Mattie pulled themselves out of the chairs. "An animal?"

Ahmad moved quickly and quietly across the room. As the noise came again, he flung the door open.

Bell stood on the step outside, dressed in a rain poncho that was longer than he was tall. Water dripped off the hood. He looked very pleased with himself.

"I woke up and you were gone!" he announced. "Don't worry—I didn't wake Mom and Da. But I looked in the windows of the wagons where lights were on, and I saw you." He pointed to a crate pushed against the side of the wagon, where he must have stood to see in the window.

Mattie sighed. "Very ingenious, Bell."

He grinned. "I *am* a genius. Can I come in? It's kind of wet out here."

Ahmad stood aside, and Bell entered, shucking off his poncho. He sat cross-legged on the carpet and picked up the empty chips bag. "You ate them all? Rats. So what are you doing here?"

Ahmad was silent. It was clear that he didn't know whether to trust Bell or not. "He's okay," Mattie told him, and to Bell she said, "We're going to get my talent back." She explained Ahmad's situation and what they'd figured out about Master Morogh.

When she was done, Bell chewed his lip for a moment. "So how can we get Master Morogh and the tigers together?" he asked. "If he's that scared of them, he's not going to go near them for anything."

They all looked at Ahmad.

"We will bring the tigers to him," Ahmad said. "We will distract him and trap him in his own lair."

Bell smiled. He liked the sound of that. But, always practical, he asked, "How do we do that?"

"Mattie must do it," Ahmad replied.

Mattie gulped. "I must?"

"Morogh is a greedy man. You must offer him something he wants."

"Something he wants?" Mattie repeated. "But he *has* what he wants! He took it from me!"

Distracted, Ahmad ran his hands through his hair. His bun came unrolled and he rolled it back up again, thinking hard. "Why does he want to read minds? What is he looking for?"

"He wants power," Selena offered. "He wants to control people. To control everything, if he can."

"So," Ahmad said, "you must make him think there is even more he can do to gain control."

"Huh," Mattie mused. "Like there's something he doesn't know. A trick, or a way to use the talent so it's even stronger."

Selena's face was anxious. "But . . . what if he touched you? He'd see what you were really thinking."

"That's true," Mattie said, a shiver moving up her spine. "I'll just have to make sure he doesn't touch me."

"Oh, Mattie!" Selena cried. "Haven't you been through enough?"

"Hey," Bell said. "Mattie's tough. She can do it."

Mattie smiled halfheartedly at him. She didn't feel very tough.

"He'll be in his office before the performance," Ahmad said. "He always takes a few minutes to himself then. That will be the time."

Mattie nodded.

"Now you must rest," Ahmad told her, and she nodded again. She was trembling with exhaustion. Or was it fear?

The rain had finally stopped. Mattie and Bell dropped Selena off at her wagon and then crept into their own, still dark and quiet. They slipped on their pajamas, and Mattie pushed her wet and borrowed clothes and Bell's poncho into an old trunk so Maya wouldn't come across them in the morning and ask questions. Then they crawled into their bunks.

Mattie was having a dream where Hasha was sitting on her stomach and licking her face. At first it was scary, but then it made her laugh because it tickled. She woke herself up laughing, and she realized when she opened her eyes that there *was* something sitting on her stomach. And something else was licking her face.

"Tibby, get off!" Mattie said, rolling her sister onto her back.

"It wasn't me, it was Tray!" Tibby said, giggling wildly and kicking Mattie. Yes, right there next to the bunk was Tray, wriggling like crazy.

"Hey, good dog," Mattie said, putting her arms around him and nuzzling his soft ears. She missed hearing his funny thoughts, but his cheerful tail told her what he felt.

"We watched you sleep!" Tibby told her.

"That must have been boring," Mattie said.

"Yeah," Tibby agreed. "But now you should get up."

Mattie sat up fast, cracking her head on the upper bunk. This made Tibby laugh, and she laughed harder when her sister scowled at her.

Mattie scrambled out of bed, rubbing her head, and got dressed quickly. "Where is everyone?"

"Outside. Mama said I could stay and watch you."

Mattie got Tibby ready to go out, and they opened the wagon door to find Da, Maya, and Bell sitting outside on the folding chairs. The day was bright and hot. The only hint of the wild storm the night before was the mud puddles on the midway, and they were quickly drying in the sun. Tray danced around them, then darted off to find Dee.

Maya handed Mattie a packet. "Here, Stewie made this for you."

Mattie unwrapped it—a ham and cheese sandwich. She was starving.

"We still haven't much of a plan," Da told her. "Only to

confront the ringmaster. Demand your talent back. I can't say what he'll do."

He'll just laugh, Mattie thought as she chewed, ravenous. Then she remembered her own plan, hatched in the night with Selena, Bell, and Ahmad. Her stomach clenched against the food and she coughed. Bell thumped her on the back.

Mattie put down her sandwich. There was no way she could eat any more. "When will you do it?"

"After the show," Da said. "The others have been grand. I dinna think they understand, truly—not all of it. But they want to help. We'll all go together."

Mattie looked at Bell, and he gave her a small, secret smile.

It was after ten, and the rest of the morning passed quickly, with preparations for the final night's performance keeping Mattie distracted. Everything that could be scrubbed, swept, and shined was. The rousties put a quick coat of paint on the Marvelwoods' wagon, making the mistake of allowing Tibby to help. Mattie spent nearly an hour trying to scrub the green off her face and out of her hair.

There was no sign of the ringmaster. His door was closed, the shades on his windows drawn. Mattie scuttled by his wagon every time she had to pass that way. She had no idea what she'd do if she saw him.

By four thirty, everyone was ready. Even the rousties had shaved and put on clean T-shirts. They gathered on the midway, and Master Morogh came to inspect them. Mattie could hardly bear to look at him.

Almost as bad were the glances everyone gave her—the clowns, Dee, all the Silvas. She could tell that everybody knew now, about the family, about what the ringmaster had done. Mattie wondered how they'd reacted when they found out. Did they think it was interesting, weird, scary that the Marvelwoods could do such bizarre things? Did they even believe it? She couldn't meet anyone's eyes. But then she saw Dee smile at her, and Bub winked. Mrs. Silva blew her a kiss, and the Bellamys gave her five discreet, identical thumbs-ups. It helped to warm the part of her that had been left cold and empty.

"Good, good, good," Master Morogh said when he'd looked everyone over. "Dee, cover those tattoos, please. It's our last night."

Dee snorted in outrage. "I will not!" she said, holding up her tattooed arms.

"You will," Master Morogh said. His tone was mild, but it clearly held a threat. Sal handed Dee a plaid, long-sleeved shirt, and she slipped it on over her tank, scowling.

"You can all understand that we must make as good an impression as we can," Master Morogh said. "We want to be invited back. Do your best, people. Do better than your best."

Mattie bit her lip. She wouldn't be doing anything. There was no way she could read clients—the Marvelwoods didn't fake it. Oh, how she hated the ringmaster!

Master Morogh turned on his heel and started toward his wagon, and Mattie gulped. It was time to put her plan into action.

"I'm going to Selena's," she said to Da. Before he could answer, she plunged into the crowd. The gates were open to the public now, and people streamed down the midway. Mattie let the movement of the crowd carry her toward the big top. Then she veered off toward Ahmad's wagon. She knocked on the door, and he opened it a crack.

"Master Morogh's going to his wagon," she said. "I'll head there now."

"Give me ten minutes," Ahmad replied. "And be sure his door is unlocked!"

The early evening heat pressed down on Mattie, though the sun was sinking toward the horizon. She could hear Dee's dogs barking in the distance as she walked to the ringmaster's wagon. She wished Tray was with her. He would give her courage.

Then she heard Bell.

"The ringmaster's got a gun," he said quietly, off to her left. "Remember? He pulled it out when the tigers were loose."

"Where are you?" Mattie hissed.

"I have my talent back, you know." His voice was right beside her. "I'll go in with you. He won't see me. I'll get the gun."

"It's too dangerous!" Mattie whispered. "I can't let you do that!"

"You can't stop me," he replied. "Don't worry. I'll be careful."

Mattie didn't want this. She was supposed to watch out for Bell. But she had no choice.

"If he gets hold of the gun, you run. Do you promise?"

"I swear it," Bell said.

She held her breath and rapped on Master Morogh's red door. The paint looked pale and washed out in the last light of day. There was no answer, so she knocked again, harder, and then the door opened.

Master Morogh stood silhouetted at the top of the wagon stairs. He seemed much larger than he really was, the way he did in the big top.

"Mattie!" he said. "Well, well, well. You should go and get a seat. The show will start soon."

"I know," Mattie said. "But I had to talk to you."

His eyes narrowed, but he said, "Ah. Then come in." He stood back, barely far enough for her to pass by without touching him. She couldn't let him touch her. She darted inside, hoping that Bell was right behind her.

The hot breeze slammed the door shut, and she noticed that Master Morogh didn't turn the lock. That was one good thing. She took a deep breath and looked around. She hadn't been in the ringmaster's wagon before.

The part of the wagon she was in looked like an office. The shades were drawn, and the interior was dark. One shade flapped against an open window above a desk that had a green-shaded lamp on top and a chair in front of it. Papers were spread all over the desktop. She thought of the gun. Where was it? And where was Bell?

Another chair was pushed against the wall, and Master Morogh motioned to it. "Sit down, Mattie," he said. He sat in the desk chair, and Mattie perched on the edge of hers. "Now, what exactly do you want? If you've come about . . . what happened yesterday, then I need to tell you, I am not making any more bargains with you. What's done is done. We came to a fair agreement."

Mattie gritted her teeth. "I know it was fair. I don't like it, but I know there's nothing I can do about it."

"Then what brings you here?" He seemed genuinely curious.

Mattie looked hard at him, trying to find in his round face with its silky pointed beard the forlorn, sobbing baby she'd seen when she touched his hand, the bleeding, dirty little boy. But even though she could read Selena a bit without her talent, she couldn't read Master Morogh at all.

"There's something you should know, something more," Mattie said. She was amazed that her voice didn't shake.

"More?"

"More to my talent. There's more you can do with it."

"Oh, really," he said. He sounded slightly interested.

"Yes," Mattie said. She got up and moved around a little. She was starting to realize that ten minutes was a very long time. "You know that if you touch someone, you can read their thoughts."

Master Morogh nodded.

"Well, if you keep holding the person, but you use two hands, and you close your eyes, then you see even more."

"What else do you see?"

"You see their deepest secrets," Mattie said. "You see what they want most to hide. Sometimes they can keep it from you at first, if they're strong, but this way, they can't hide anything." She had spent a long time coming up with this idea as she moved the broom in the dust around the wagon and scrubbed green paint off Tibby. There was a little bit of truth in it—the idea that it was possible to see more than just surface thoughts. She hoped that would make it sound more believable.

Master Morogh was silent. Would he believe her?

"Ahhh," he said at last. He drew the sound out. It was clear he really liked this idea. His eyes were shining. But then they clouded.

"And why are you telling me this, Mattie my girl?" he asked. "I can't imagine it's because you're so fond of me."

"I despise you," Mattie said clearly. "But my parents need this job. They need to stay with your circus. And they were afraid that after—after everything, you'd fire them. We don't have anywhere else to go."

The ringmaster was quiet, so Mattie went on. "You said no bargains, so I just gave you this, for free. If you want to give

167

us something yourself in return, well . . . you can keep us on."
She looked at the floor. She had no idea if he would find this
convincing.

"I see, I see, I see," Master Morogh murmured. "Well, your
father and mother and brother are a reliable draw, a definite
attraction. But you, now—you're not so very useful without
your talent, are you?"

Mattie winced at his cruelty. She supposed it was payback
for her *I despise you*. She couldn't help looking up at him. She
didn't know what exactly showed in her eyes, but he smiled,
and his smile raised goose bumps on her arms.

"I thank you for the information," he said, rising from his
chair. "Now, shall we test your claim? What secrets are you
holding deep in your devious little mind, Mattie Marvelwood?"

He pulled off both gloves and held out his hands, and
Mattie backed away from him. There wasn't much space in
the wagon, and she pressed herself against the far wall as he
advanced. Her heart was hammering so hard that it shook her
with each beat.

She tried to make her mind a blank. She knew that as soon
as Master Morogh touched her, he'd see her plan. He wouldn't
even have to look deep to read it. He came closer and closer,
his hands outstretched, and she thought *nothing nothing nothing*
as hard as she could. But of course it didn't work. Her mind
was full of tigers—tigers and revenge—and when his hands
came down on her shoulders, he saw it all. His face, close
enough to hers that she could feel his breath, contorted with
fury.

The ringmaster dropped his hands and spun, heading
toward his desk. Mattie realized that the gun must be in one
of the drawers, and she clutched at his arm as he passed. When

he tried to pull away from her she saw, out of the corner of her eye, the desk drawer sliding open. Bell! Then the gun, thrown by Bell's invisible hand, arced through the air and out the open window, making the shade flap and landing with a thump in the dirt outside the wagon.

Master Morogh let out a bellow of rage, a shout so furious that Mattie sprang away from him in fright. The ringmaster grabbed her but tripped, falling into his desk and tipping over the lamp, which fell to the floor with a crash. The bulb shattered, and the wagon, its window shades pulled down, was plunged into darkness. And a second later there was another crash: the door of the wagon flying open as Ahmad and his tigers made their entrance.

CHAPTER 17

Ahmad and the big cats were inside in a minute, and Ahmad slammed the wagon door shut. It was so dark without the lamp that Mattie wasn't sure at first if her eyes were open or closed. She struggled with the ringmaster in the pitch blackness, but with his weightlifter's strength, stolen from some poor circus bodybuilder years before, he was much stronger than she was. He swung behind her and locked his arm around her neck, holding her in front of him like a shield. She could feel him trembling.

She heard the soft padding of the tigers' paws on the wood floor of the wagon as they advanced, and she smelled their musky odor. But she couldn't see a thing.

"Call them off, Ahmad," Master Morogh ordered, his

words loud in her ear. "I've got Mattie, and they'll have to go through her to get to me."

Ahmad's voice came from the far side of the wagon. It was calm and amused. "Oh, they will eat you from the feet up without touching Mattie," he said. "By the time they get to your knees, you will let her go."

"I'll break her neck," Master Morogh threatened. "Call them off!" He tightened his arm, and despite herself, Mattie yelped. She remembered that he'd threatened Ahmad's son with his gun. But would he actually kill a person? Kill *her*?

Quickly Ahmad said something in his language, and the tigers' movement stopped. There was absolute stillness, utter silence. In the terrible quiet, Mattie couldn't even hear the sound of breathing. She waited, not knowing what she was waiting for.

Then out of the darkness a bright light flashed just above her head, exactly where the ringmaster's face was. Bell shouted, "Mattie, go!"

Master Morogh's grip loosened just a little in his surprise, and Mattie wrenched herself out of his grasp. In the light she could see Bell, visible again, standing by the door. He held his little army knife flashlight, aiming its beam straight at Master Morogh's eyes. It had blinded him for an instant—just long enough for her to break free.

The ringmaster reached out to grab her again, but she darted between the tigers and ran to the other end of the wagon, glass from the broken lamp crunching under her feet. She cowered beside the desk. Bell kept the flashlight trained on Master Morogh as the tigers moved toward him. The ringmaster backed away, pressing himself against the wall as if he thought he could push right through it. His face was twisted with terror. Mattie almost felt sorry for him—almost.

"Call them off, Ahmad," the ringmaster said once more, but now it was a plea.

Ahmad said something else, and the tigers halted again. Their tails switched back and forth. Their eyes were fastened on Master Morogh. In the thin beam of the flashlight Mattie could see sweat beaded on his forehead.

"I *could* call them off, Morogh," Ahmad said serenely. "You see that they will do as I ask."

"Yes, yes, yes," Master Morogh snarled. Hadi obviously didn't like his tone, because he growled a little, deep in his throat. More quietly, almost meekly, the ringmaster said, "What is it that you want? What will it take?"

"You threatened my son," Ahmad said. "You have kept me away from my family for many years. How shall these wrongs be righted?"

"Whatever you want," Master Morogh begged. "I'll do anything you say."

Just at the edge of the flashlight's beam Mattie saw Hasha bend forward to sniff Master Morogh's feet, and the ringmaster let out a mouselike squeak. Then the tiger raised one of her thick paws with its razor-sharp claws. She ran a claw slowly down the ringmaster's midsection from neck to belly, popping the buttons on his starched white shirt. The cats were playing with him, like a housecat might play with a mouse before eating it. Although Mattie could see out of the corner of her eye that it made Bell grin with delight, she was starting to feel bad. She'd read enough people's thoughts to know that everyone was afraid of something, just as everyone had secrets. Making someone's worst fear come true was an awful thing to do. Even if that someone was Master Morogh.

"Tell him what we want, Ahmad," she said.

Ahmad looked surprised and a little disappointed, but he nodded. "All right," he said. "You must give back Mattie's power, and my own."

"Give back Mattie's power?" Master Morogh repeated. "Mattie, is that truly what you want?"

"Well . . . of course it is," Mattie said, confused.

"But now you are like everyone else. With your talent, you will be different again. You will be so very odd."

Mattie remembered what he'd said when he took her talent. *You don't like to be different.* When he'd touched her, he knew it was true. He'd seen her feelings and thoughts.

"The others will make fun of you, as they did me. They'll mock you. They'll tease you. They'll beat you bloody. You'll never fit in. Never, never, never." His voice had become low and hypnotic.

"I don't care!" Mattie exclaimed. It wasn't true. She did care. It was hard to be different—to be one of the freak family. But now she knew that it was far worse not to be. "It's what I want."

"But . . . ," Master Morogh said slowly, "I read your mind yesterday, behind the wagons. You didn't want your talent anymore. Your thoughts can't lie." He sounded truly bewildered.

Mattie stepped forward a little so he could see her in the beam of the flashlight.

"Thoughts can't lie," she acknowledged. "But they can change. Reading minds is a little like what my mother does when she sees the future. She sees what will happen if someone doesn't change. That's why she's always warning people. What I see—what you saw in me—are thoughts that can change. If the person thinking them changes."

Hadi snarled again, and Master Morogh winced.

"I want you to give my talent back," Mattie said firmly. "And the others, all the others. The singer Julietta, the ringmaster. Ahmad. All the people you hypnotized. Give back what you took from all of them."

The ringmaster gritted his teeth. Hasha bent forward once more, and her long tongue came out and licked Master Morogh's shiny boot.

"Yes!" he cried. "I will, I will, I will!"

"Swear it," Mattie insisted. "Swear it on your life."

"I swear it on my life!"

"And how can I know that you won't do it again? To other people? Will you swear you won't take anything from anyone else?"

Master Morogh grimaced. He hadn't expected that.

"But I'll have nothing," he said. His voice was faint.

"You'll have what's yours," Mattie said. "You'll have your ability to hypnotize, and nothing more. Now swear it."

"That's only a trick, it's not a talent," the ringmaster objected. "Not like yours."

"It's all you get," Mattie said.

The ringmaster hesitated, and the tigers stepped forward. Now their heads were almost pressed against him. They growled softly, a low rumble. Master Morogh moaned.

"I . . . swear it," he managed. "I swear it on my life!"

"And one last thing," Mattie said. "You have to go."

"Go?"

"Leave the circus. Go away. Leave these people alone."

"But . . . but the circus is mine," Master Morogh protested. "It's been mine for years and years. It's my livelihood, my life. That's not fair. I don't deserve that."

"How can you say that?" Mattie demanded. "You've

injured people—you've ruined their lives! You deserve worse. You know you do."

"If you let me stay, I will be only the owner, no more. I won't interfere, I promise." Master Morogh sounded sincere, and Mattie felt her resolve wavering for a moment. But then she thought of what he'd done to Selena and Bell and Maya. Of the gun and Ahmad's son. She shook her head.

"Nobody trusts you," she said. "We can't take that risk."

The ringmaster hesitated, his lips pursed. Hasha pushed her head against his chest, rubbing gently as if she were scratching an itch. He gave a little yelp.

"I swear it," he said, his voice low and trembling. "On my life."

"All right. Do it now," Mattie commanded him.

"Please," he said. "Call them off." Mattie nodded at Ahmad, and he spoke again. The tigers took a step backward.

The ringmaster closed his eyes and held his ungloved hands out. The cats tensed, but they didn't move. Mattie got the impression that Hasha really wanted those other fingers.

Then something happened that Mattie would never know afterward how to describe. It was like a wave moving through the wagon—a wave of air, or of something indefinable. It washed over them—first over the tigers, making their tails twitch. It reached Ahmad, standing behind the cats, and he stumbled and fell to his knees. Bell leaned back and then forward in its wake, making the flashlight beam waver wildly, and finally it hit Mattie.

Like Ahmad, Mattie dropped to her knees, struck by both the force of the wave and the enormous feeling of relief it brought. It was her talent, her power, her *self* flowing over her and into her. He'd really done it. Master Morogh had given her self back to her. For a long moment she knelt there, as the hole in her center filled slowly with joy.

"Mattie!" Bell said, helping her to her feet. "Are you okay?"

"I'm good," Mattie said. "I'm good!"

Hasha and Hadi had turned away from Master Morogh. It was obvious that he was no concern of theirs anymore. They nuzzled Ahmad almost like housecats would, and he put a hand on each of their heads. He closed his eyes and smiled, the first time Mattie had ever seen him smile.

"Am I free to leave?" Master Morogh said. He tried to make the words sound casual as he picked his gloves up from the floor.

"Get out," Ahmad said. The tigers ignored the ringmaster as he made his way toward the door and turned the knob.

"And where do you think you're going, then?" It was Da's voice. The wagon door swung open, but darkness had fallen outside, and Mattie couldn't see anything.

"Da!" Mattie called out, and Bell aimed the flashlight toward the door. There was their father, holding the gun that Bell had tossed out the window, and next to him was Maya, her black hair wild. Behind them were the other members of the circus—every last one of them, it looked like. The Bellamys and the Silvas, Dee and the clowns, all the rousties, crowding around the steps that led to the wagon door.

"What on earth is going on?" Maya exclaimed.

Da held up his own flashlight and shone it inside. It was a lot more powerful than Bell's. Everything—Master Morogh, the two tigers, the broken lamp, Ahmad and Bell and Mattie— showed in its glow. Maya let out a strangled cry.

"The tigers!" she shouted. "Get away from the tigers!"

Mattie ran to the door. "It's okay, Maya," she said. "We're

safe. We're fine. We just . . ." Then she stopped. It was a little hard to explain what had happened.

"What are you up to, Morogh?" Da demanded.

Master Morogh blinked in the light. "I was just leaving," he said.

"Wait a minute—," Da said.

"No, let him go, Da," Mattie interrupted. "We got it all back. He's given us back what he stole. He's going—for good."

"Going? Going where? What's happening here? Mattie—"

"It doesn't matter where," Mattie told him. "It's over. He's done. Let him go."

Something in her tone convinced him, and he stepped aside. Master Morogh started down the stairs, pulling on his gloves. He didn't seem tall and threatening, the way he had in the big top. He didn't have the old ringmaster's presence now, or any of the skills and powers he'd taken from people over the years. He was just a short, round little man in a funny outfit. He didn't look at anyone. Mattie could tell that he wanted to seem jaunty and untroubled, but his beard trembled and he almost tripped. The others moved to let him by. In silence they gazed after him as he walked away.

A sliver of moon peeked through the clouds. Mattie watched Master Morogh stumble down the midway to the gate at the entrance of the circus lot. He passed under the sign. Then she couldn't see him anymore.

CHAPTER 18

"M arvelwood!"

Mattie turned. It was Mr. Silva, Selena beside him.

"What'll we do now?" Mr. Silva asked. "The audience is waiting!"

The audience. Mattie shook her head hard, trying to bring herself back to the present. There was a tent full of people. There was no ringmaster, no one to introduce the acts. And they couldn't possibly send everyone away. It would be a disaster. Word would get out, and it would be the ruin of the circus.

Da and Mr. Silva conferred as the others ran toward the big top to get their acts ready.

"Did it work?" Selena cried, throwing her arms around Mattie. "Are you all right? What happened?"

With her touch Mattie felt worry. Fear. Love. She could read her friend. Oh, it was so wonderful!

"It worked," she said. "He's gone. And I'm back." Selena stepped back quickly, then grinned and gave Mattie another hug.

"You can read me all you want," she said. "I'm just so glad for you!"

"Selena!" Mr. Silva said. "Run to our wagon and get my cutaway from the closet. Hurry!"

"You mean that fancy jacket?" Selena said. "But we don't use that one in this act."

"It's for Simon," Mr. Silva said. "He'll be ringmaster tonight."

Mattie stared at Da, and he smiled at her. "I'll stick a few illusions in," he said. "The audience won't miss Morogh one bit."

"Simon, that is too dangerous!" Maya protested. "Illusions, in front of so many? You'll be found out!"

"Nonsense," Da said. "They'll all think it's a trick. Mirrors or some such. None of them has a big enough imagination to suspect the truth."

Maya shook her head doubtfully, but it was clear to Mattie that it would be Da's show. He put on the jacket that Selena brought a moment later, and though they all laughed at the sequins and jeweled buttons that covered it, Mattie thought he looked pretty impressive.

Mattie, Bell, Tibby, and Maya entered the big top through the front, while the Silvas and Da went in through the back. When they'd found places to sit in the straw, Mattie looked around.

On the bleachers she saw Audra and her grandchildren, there for a second time, and not far from Audra sat the kids Mattie had insulted in the diner. Mattie waved to Audra, and then to the kids. Audra gave her a big smile. The boys ignored her, but after a minute the girl raised her hand in a tiny acknowledgement.

Then the lights went down, and the show began.

Da was great. It was like he'd been born to be a ringmaster. He announced each act with a little illusion of it—a wavering vision of the clowns on their unicycles, the Silvas bowing, Pinga lifting her trunk. And the artistes gave what Mattie was sure were their best performances ever. Selena, her grace back, somersaulted through the air not once but twice, and both were perfect. Mattie clapped until her hands were sore, and so did the rest of the audience.

When the show was over, the artistes stood in two rows, and the audience passed between them, congratulating them and shaking their hands. Audra stopped in front of Mattie, holding a little boy and girl by the hand. They had her curly hair and bright eyes.

"Your daddy did a fine job in there!" she said. "I've never seen anything like it. Those hologram things were just beautiful. I hope y'all come back next summer. You've been great for business!"

Mattie smiled but didn't answer.

"Give us a hug, honey," Audra said, and she pulled Mattie to her with strong, soft arms. Mattie flinched, but the thoughts she read at Audra's touch were full of kindness. "Y'all have a good winter, now!" Audra told her.

"You, too," Mattie said. Audra and her grandchildren joined a group of other white-haired women and they headed out the gate. *I hope y'all come back next summer.* Mattie sighed.

When the audience had dispersed and all the cars were gone from the lot, the dust settled slowly and the rousties and artistes began the pull-down—the dismantling of the circus.

It didn't take nearly as long as Mattie had thought it would. Before midnight, everything was packed in wagons, ready to leave in the morning. Da said they would be heading west—maybe all the way to California, if the truck could make it. The rest of the circus was going south.

Though it was late, the rousties built one last bonfire. There was no dancing; all the instruments had been packed, and everyone was exhausted. Mattie huddled close to Bell, looking around at the people they'd grown so close to in such a short time. She could tell that they all knew exactly what had happened, and she wondered how. They'd only been there for the last moments. But then Selena came over to Mattie and said, "I told people what went on in Master Morogh's wagon. Or, anyway, I told some of it. And Ahmad told the rest."

"What did they say?" Mattie asked.

Selena squinched her face up, remembering. "Let's see . . . Oto said, 'She's a brave one, that Mattie!' And Dee danced around with the dogs until Blanch got dizzy and fell over. And Bub threw Winston up in the air and scared him so badly he pooped on Solomon's head."

Mattie had to laugh. "So they're all glad Master Morogh's gone?" She didn't even like to say his name.

"Nobody liked him," Selena said. "He was creepy and horrible and a thief."

"And a bampot," Tibby muttered, and Selena laughed, too.

"Yes, the worst bampot ever!" Selena agreed.

Stewie handed around sausages roasted on sticks, and Mattie ate hungrily. As she chewed, Mr. Silva stood up in front of the fire and clapped his hands to get people's attention.

"Things have changed for the Circus of Wonders," he said. "Morogh is gone—gone for good, I'm pretty sure." There was a cheer, and the dogs, sitting next to Stewie in the hope of snatching a sausage, started barking.

"He left all his account books, and I've taken a quick look over the numbers. They're not in terrible shape. It doesn't seem like it would be an impossibility for us to buy him out."

"You mean buy the circus ourselves?" Maso Bellamy said. "We'd be the owners?"

"All of us," Mr. Silva replied. "We'd each put in what we could, and we'd own that percentage of it. It would be ours legally."

"What about Morogh?" Dee asked. "What if he refused?"

"We'd use lawyers. I found his lawyer's name in his papers. Wherever he's gone, I'm sure they could get in touch with him. We'd pay what the circus was worth. I'm willing to bet he won't object, considering . . . everything."

Everyone started talking at once. The general sense Mattie got was that people liked this idea a lot. But it was kind of hard to tell.

"Hey," Dee said, then yelled, "Hey!" The troupe quieted down. "We're not the most organized group. Maybe we could have a president? Or a leader, anyway? Silva, will you do it?"

People clapped and shouted, and the dogs barked some more. Mr. Silva accepted the job. Then Ahmad spoke up in his lilting voice. Everyone quieted to hear him.

"I cannot stay. I must get back to my family. And my cats must go as well."

"That'll be a real loss," Mr. Silva said. "The audience loves those cats."

Ahmad was silent, and Mr. Silva sighed. "Of course you have to go. But how are you going to get the tigers back? The airlines probably won't let them on." He was joking, but Ahmad's face was somber.

"I cannot see a way to get them back. They have to stay here. But they must be free."

"Stay here?" Mrs. Silva said. "In South Carolina?"

Mattie remembered what Ahmad had told her about letting the tigers out, and she said, "It's a lot like where they come from, right, Ahmad?"

"Yes," he said. "The woodland here"—he swung his arm, indicating the trees on the other side of the wooden fence outside—"it is swamp forest, just like our forest at home, with the same sort of prey they are used to. They could do well here."

"But if anyone ever saw them . . . ," Oto mused. Mattie shuddered, imagining the terror people would feel, the frantic hunt through the swamp for the cats.

"I have spoken to them," Ahmad said. "They know the dangers. They will take care."

"You've spoken to them?" Mr. Silva repeated. He shook his head and laughed, and for the second time Mattie saw Ahmad smile.

"And Hasha is too old now to have cubs. So there will not be more. They will be the only ones."

"That's sad," Selena said. "They'll be all alone."

Mattie remembered the images Hasha had shown her of cubs frolicking, and nodded. "But it's better that way. If there was a whole family of tigers, people would definitely notice."

Ahmad agreed. "With only two, it will be far safer. And there is no animal better at not being noticed than a tiger, if that is what it wants."

"Do it," Dee said. "Set them free. None of us will say anything. We'll find an act to replace them."

"How about a human cannonball?" Oto suggested. Tibby's mouth dropped open, her bicolored eyes round.

"Or a fire-eater?" said Negyed.

"A contortionist!" cried Maso.

"Knife throwers!" That was Harma.

"Jugglers!" added Elso.

The clowns were offended. "Hey, *we* juggle," Chaz protested.

"But badly," Oto said, grinning, and Chaz lunged for him as Winston flapped off his shoulder and squawked, "Behave, gentlemen!"

"And you, Ahmad, how will you get back?" Mr. Silva asked, once they'd settled down again.

"Morogh and the tigers and I came by cargo ship," Ahmad said. "We arrived secretly, by night. I will go to Charleston and try to find passage back the same way."

"I know a guy at the shipyards," Bub said. "I'll give you his name, and he'll set you up."

Ahmad bowed his head. "I would be grateful," he said.

"And what about Pinga?" Mr. Silva asked. "Should we let her go as well?"

Dee shook her head. "Pinga's old, and all she's ever known is the circus. I think she likes it with us."

"I know she does," Mattie assured her, remembering what she'd seen when she touched the elephant. "She's happy here— as long as she doesn't have to give too many people rides."

"Maybe I should retire her," Dee said with a sigh. "She's earned a rest. But if I do, I'll definitely have to get more dogs!"

"There's one other thing," Mr. Silva said. He looked at Maya and Da. "We'd like you Marvelwoods to stay on."

Mattie drew in a sharp breath. Da didn't look surprised at all, though Maya, sitting across the table, did. Alarm, anxiety, and fear chased each other across her face. But there was something else there, too. A sort of . . . longing?

"We think you'd be a wonderful addition to the circus," Mrs. Silva said gently to Maya, patting her shoulder. Maya winced at the touch but didn't shy away. "We'd love to have you stay."

Maya bit her lip. Mattie wondered if she was thinking about Odelle, who'd been a friend, too, and betrayed her so terribly. She understood now how scary it was for Maya to trust someone.

"Maya love," Da said, reaching across the table for her hand, "it would be good for all of us, I think. We could settle down for a bit."

Maya looked at her family for a long moment. It was obvious what Mattie and Bell felt. And Tibby bounced up and down on the bench and cried, "Let's stay with the circus! Let's stay with the dogs and Pinga and all five twins!"

"Well," Maya said at last, careful as always, "we could try it. We could see how it goes."

Selena gave a great hoot of delight and sprang up, and Mattie jumped up, too, and threw her arms around her friend. Selena's thoughts were pure joy, and Mattie's were, too. The others all crowded around, shaking hands and whacking the Marvelwoods on the back. Bell was so happy he disappeared without even meaning to and reappeared a moment later looking surprised at himself. Dee was the only one who noticed, and she laughed until she had to hold her stomach.

"You Marvelwoods!" she cried. "Oh, we'll have a circus like no other!"

"Hey," Sal the roustie said, "I hate to interrupt all this sweetness and light, but if we're gonna make it even halfway to Florida tomorrow we've got to get some rest."

"Florida?" Mattie said to Selena.

"The season's over, silly," Selena told her. "It's September. We winter in Gibsonton. We get little jobs there, weekend gigs sometimes. But that's where we live, all of us. That's where the beach is, and our house, and my school."

School. Mattie's face must have looked just like Maya's had, because Selena squeezed her arm. "Don't fret about that, pilgrim,'" she said in a gravelly voice. It was another of her John Wayne lines. "You'll be with me. We'll be brilliant together."

Mattie took a deep breath. She'd wanted to go to school forever. How much scarier than facing down Master Morogh could it be?

She thought about what Audra had said that afternoon at the diner. *We just have to try for gratitude. To realize when we have enough.* The circus, Selena, a house in Florida. Her family. That was more than enough. She could be grateful for those things. She'd work on being grateful for school later.

In the morning, before they left Frog Creek, they freed the tigers. The entire troupe, rousties and all, walked to their wagon. Everyone stood well back as Ahmad urged the cats out. Hadi came first, proud and sleek, and Hasha after him, her tail twitching and her ears turning this way and that like little radars. People shrank away from them still, but Mattie knew they wouldn't hurt anyone.

The troupe walked out the front gate of the lot and around the fence to the place where the forest started. "It goes for miles and miles," Ahmad said. "They'll have plenty of room to get lost—and stay lost."

Then he called Mattie over. "I have said my farewells already. But will you say good-bye, Mattie?"

"Mattie . . . ," Maya said anxiously, but Mattie ignored her mother. She walked forward.

When she got near the tigers, she knelt down. Hadi took no notice of her, but Hasha padded over. She lowered her head, and Mattie placed her hand on the soft fur between the tiger's ears. She could feel a warm pulse beat beneath her palm. She saw the same images she'd seen when she touched Hasha before: sunny glades and pools of water, trees and vines, a sense of peace.

"Yes," Mattie whispered to the tiger, gazing into her amber eyes. "It can be like that, if you're careful. Be careful. Be safe. Good-bye!"

Then the tigers crouched at the edge of the woods, and Ahmad spoke. They were off like a shot. Almost instantly their striped coats vanished into the forest's stripes of sun and shade. Ahmad lifted his hand to his face. His back was to Mattie, and she thought maybe he was wiping away tears. When he turned around again, though, his eyes were shining with gladness.

Ahmad had brought a backpack. He slung it over his shoulder, and Mattie went up to him and hugged him. At first he was stiff in her embrace, but then his arms went around her, too. "Thank you," she said. She wanted to say a lot more than that, but she couldn't find the words.

"Thank *you*," he replied, and Mattie could tell that he meant more by it as well. She couldn't read him, now that he had his talent back, but she could tell that he was eager, and nervous, too.

"It'll be fine," she told him. "Your family will be so glad to see you!" He smiled—the third time in two days!—and shook everyone's hand. And then he, too, was gone, disappearing down the road that led to Frog Creek, the same road that had brought Mattie and her family to the circus, just over a week before.

The others started back into the lot to their trucks and wagons, but Mattie stood in the warm sunshine gazing after Ahmad. He had such a long way to go. Would his little boy remember him?

"Come along, Mattie," Maya said, her tone scolding. "We have to finish packing up. Right now."

"Yes," Mattie said, turning around. "I'm coming, I'm coming. Stop nagging me!"

Maya opened her mouth, ready to snap back at her, but Mattie put up her hands and said, "Joking! I was just joking!"

Maya's lips turned up just a little. "And I did not mean to nag," she said. At Mattie's expression of stunned surprise, she broke into her full-on, hundred-watt Maya smile, and Mattie rolled her eyes and began to laugh. Bell grinned at Mattie, and Tibby grabbed her hand and pulled her forward.

The freak family was on the move again.

But this time, the freak family was going home.

ACKNOWLEDGMENTS

My heartfelt thanks to:

MARY COLGAN, who turns out to be the editor I always wanted

JENNIFER LAUGHRAN, who found the Marvelwoods a home

SHANI SOLOFF, whose idea it was

BEN SICKER, who thought of Sumatran tigers

PETER ZAHLER, who knows what Sumatran tigers eat without even looking it up

KATHY ZAHLER, who sympathizes when I whinge

JAN ZAHLER, who believes I can do anything

DEBRA AND ARNIE CARDILLO, who are the best collaborators

JINX the circus dog

and, always,

PHIL SICKER, whose talent is love

31901063198578